Between Today and Someday

by

Ann M. Trader

The Wonder of Wildflowers Series

Cover Art by *The Wild Rose Press, Inc.*

The Wild Rose Press, Inc.
PO Box 708
Adams Basin, NY 14410-0708
Visit us at www.thewildrosepress.com

Publishing History
First Edition, 2025
Trade Paperback ISBN 978-1-5092-6090-4
Digital ISBN 978-1-5092-6091-1

The Wonder of Wildflowers Series
Published in the United States of America

Dedication

For wildflowers like Prim, remember…your someday is
just around the corner.

Chapter One

Thursday, August 4th 8:40 a.m.
Prim

"Can't do it." I shook my head, grabbing a handful of alcohol wipes and a box of latex gloves from the supply cabinet. I dropped them into the slots on my nurse's cart before reaching for a pack of gauze. "Believe me, I understand. I know it's your wedding reception, but I can't just hop on stage with your cousin's band and fill in for their singer. That takes hours of practice. Have you forgotten you're getting married in two days?"

Tiffany folded her arms across her middle. "Come on, Prim. She's their *backup* singer." She tilted her head to the side, just enough to make her short ponytail bounce. "And besides, your voice is a thousand times better than hers."

I chuckled, thinking Tiffany was a skilled nurse…and the consummate southern-girl charmer. When I'd been in serious need of a life reset two months ago, I requested a transfer from my hospital in Raleigh, North Carolina, to its regional branch in my hometown, Vista Falls, some forty miles away. Tiffany gave me a present on my first day—a red travel coffee mug with "Because my patients need my patience, bring on the coffee" printed in bold white letters. I knew I liked her right from the start.

I also discovered I liked working in a smaller hospital, one with an emergency department that hummed like a well-oiled tractor. I preferred the caseload of sprains and broken bones, varying degrees of hypertension, and the occasional food poisoning to the overdoses and assault wounds we treated in the city.

I reached for my "Patient Patience" mug sitting in the cup holder on my cart and took a sip. If I was going to hold my ground, I needed caffeine. "Sorry, but the answer is still no."

"Seriously?" Tiffany groaned a sigh. "But you sing in front of people every Sunday morning with the church choir."

The pleading in her voice was commendable, but she must have forgotten about my five siblings. Guilting didn't work on me.

I looked up, gripping the edges of my cart. "Oh, please. Those are hymns, and me and everyone else knows them by heart."

I watched Tiffany pull her lip between her teeth. "You saw the band's singer, right?"

"That doesn't change—"

"Did you hear she's now on record for being the hospital's worst allergic reaction to a bee sting? As in *ever*?" She rubbed her fingers in circles over her temples. "It'll be days before the swelling goes down and her voice recovers. There's like no way she'll be able to sing at my reception."

I touched Tiffany's arm and gave it a gentle squeeze. I dug a little deeper, hoping an explanation might help. "You're getting married on Saturday. I'm going to my Mom's tonight for a family dinner. I work all day tomorrow. There's no time for me to rehearse with the band, learn their songs—"

"Okay, okay," she said with a wave of her hand. "That's fair, I guess." Her brow wrinkled for a few long moments…until it didn't. A slow smile began to pink her cheeks, and her eyes brightened. "Prim…?"

Uh-oh.

"I totally get it. You're right—it'd be asking way too much for you to learn all her vocals." She stepped toward me and clasped my arms. "But would you please, please, *please* consider doing just one song?"

Now I was biting *my* lip.

"It's mine and Brent's song for the first dance. It's the only one where she was going to take the lead vocal. It'd be absolutely amazing if you'd do this one little thing for me." Tiffany flashed me the most heart-tugging puppy dog look—even better than the one my youngest sister did. Without missing a beat, she told me the name of the song.

At least it's one I know.

She grabbed her phone and began typing, pressing send to share the website where I could download the music.

My resolve cracked ever so slightly. I closed my eyes briefly then opened them before giving her a nod. "Okay. This one song. I'll do it for *you*."

Tiffany released a happy squeal, wrapping me in a hug, thanking me for saving the day.

I smiled as my friend practically skipped over to the nurses' station. *I'll practice at Mom's tonight.* I gave my ponytail a little tug before heading toward the triage rooms. *One song for the happy couple. No problem.*

****

After my shift ended, I went to the house, grabbed a

quick shower, and slipped on a lavender sundress. As I stood at the bedroom mirror combing my hair, my gaze followed the string of pink rosettes in the wallpaper. Despite Mom's insistence I could simply move back to the farm, I decided to rent this cute mother-in-law cottage from one of our pediatricians. It was three blocks from the hospital and a comfortable fifteen miles from Three Creeks—the working farm that'd been in my family since the eighteenth century. After the disaster of my last relationship, I wanted to live closer to my family again, just not *too* close.

Though the décor was dated—smokey blue kitchen countertops and tan paneling in the den—the cottage checked my most important boxes. *Clean, affordable, and available.* As I wrapped the curling iron around sections of my hair, a sobering thought filtered through my mind. This rental mirrored every dating relationship I'd ever had. All five had been "no deposit, no lease" short-term arrangements.

Now there's *a box I could do without checking.*

I dipped my fingers in styling gel and smoothed them over an unruly tress…and an even unrulier thought. I'd been a fool to believe I'd broken the cycle with my last boyfriend. Avery Smith-Stanton was intelligent and charming, and with his unbridled attention, I was downloading engagement apps and following bridal influencers in no time. Turned out his interest was a mask for deeper secrets.

Avery did a real number on me, but with counseling and my belief in the general goodness of most people, I was moving on. I still hoped for a loving marriage and children like my parents and sisters had, but my timeline was shrinking.

I'm thirty-one. No pressure or anything…

After a handful of cleansing breaths, I met my reflection in the mirror. For a little fortification, I brushed on a pink blush and matching lip gloss, then tossed my hair behind my shoulders and headed out the door.

****

I arrived at the family farm just as my older brothers, Ace and Thorne, were putting the chicken breasts on the grill. Ace was only sixteen months older than Thorne, and they were my best buddies and protectors for the first six years of my life. After us, Goldie came along and then the twins—Sage and Billie—joined us two years later. From then on, the Vreeland kids really were a bunch of wonderous wildflowers.

After squeezing me inside one of their taco hugs, I grabbed a beer from the cooler and the dishes from the outdoor cupboard. I fanned a tablecloth over the patio table, pressed out a few creases, and reached for the cutlery tray.

Ace popped open a beer. "Hey. I ran into Chase Bova yesterday. I didn't know he'd moved back home, was stepping back from Chase n' Dreams."

The forks and spoons in my hands clattered to the table. I peeked at my brothers from beneath my lashes, glad the song playing on the wireless speaker masked the noise. I lifted my beer to my lips, turning my ear in their direction.

"So, how come you didn't say anything?"

"Because I sit around doing nothing all day, right?" Thorne snorted. "Between your renovations and my own clients, I've barely had time to take a shit for weeks."

I swallowed a laugh. Thorne was meticulous when

it came to work, turning over every stone, crossing every T. He was an honest-to-goodness perfectionist.

Ace scrubbed his hand over his neck. "The Old Rambler farmhouse, the cottages. You've done an incredible job."

His "yeah, right" carried over a chuckle.

"No, I mean it. Your vision—what you can do with a restoration, the way you preserve all the things that make it special—makes all of us jealous."

I watched Thorne smile a thanks and grab the tongs. "So, yeah. Chase. He just got into town last week. We had a couple beers the other night." He lifted the lid on the grill, backing away from the smoke. "And get this— he's not just stepping back. He actually sold his majority interest in the company to his partners. He'll be their executive producer from now on, and still promoting in the media."

Ace furrowed his brow. "But why would he leave now? I mean, he's a celebrity who gets to fish. All. Day. Long."

"True," Thorne said, in between flipping chicken breasts. "But there's a whole lot of bullshit he had to go through to get to the fishing. He said he was ready for a change; has other things he wants to work on."

"Right. I follow his accounts." Ace pulled on his beer. "Traveling the country, fishing the best bodies of water with the best equipment money can buy, and schmoozing with sponsors *had* to be torture."

Thorne chuckled, scratching his chin with the back of his hand. "Can you believe my best friend has a quarter million followers on his channel, and even more on RugRog? Fucking crazy."

"Again, his life sucks balls. But hey, this is Chase

we're talking about. He's always been a smart guy. Bet he made a heap of money on the deal, too." A phone rang, and Ace glanced at his screen. "Sorry, man. It's Megan," he said, stepping away and walking into the house.

I tilted my head back and swallowed deeply. When I came up for air, I dabbed a drop of beer from the corner of my mouth. Chase Bova left Vista Falls more than a dozen years ago, and now he was back. Successful prodigal son returns to his hometown.

Flip a pancake…

Though lost in a brain fog, I finished setting the table, then slid into an empty chair. I gazed at Thorne as he turned the chicken, adding four ears of corn to the grill before closing the lid. He turned, flashing me his can't-forget-you smile, reminding me of the time he trick-or-treated for me—a sack in each hand—because I was home sick with strep throat. He never cared what candy he got, trading out with Ace or me just to make us smile.

Because Thorne was *that* brother who never left anyone out, I wasn't surprised when he asked, "Isn't it great Chase is home?"

I hesitated, but not because I needed him to repeat the question. I just didn't know how to give it an honest answer. So, I muttered something cordial and let out a relieved breath when he turned back to the grill.

I shifted in my chair and gazed at the sturdy oak tree some thirty feet away, recalling the summer when I was eight years old, and how Dad helped Thorne and Chase build a treehouse in it.

It was the most spectacular thing I'd ever seen, but Thorne didn't flash me his can't-forget-you smile when it came to The Hideout. He and Chase were best friends, blood brothers, and in complete agreement it was off limits to me and my kind—*girls*.

All summer long, if those two weren't fishing or playing video games or doing chores, they were in their treehouse. And I was the nerdy little sister in long braids and cut off shorts. I spent many afternoons camped out in the shade of the magnolia trees, doodling in my blue sequined diary, imagining all the fun they were having.

Until Ace and Thorne went to summer camp for a week in July....

Yes, I defied the order and climbed up to the treehouse the day after they left.

Yes, I made it to the top and took in my fill of the mysterious "no girls" refuge.

No, curiosity didn't kill the cat—but it almost broke my arm—because Chase happened along the very moment my foot slipped on the ladder on my way down. He broke my fall, catching me in his arms, and even with the wind knocked out of my lungs, I hadn't been scared. Not even for one moment...

The sizzling sound from the grill grabbed my attention. With the sunlight dipping behind the trees, I slid my sunglasses on top of my head to get a better look at my brother. *I wonder if Chase ever told him about my stunt.* A sigh escaped my lips as I realized I didn't even know how long Chase had held me that day—couldn't have been more than a dozen seconds. *A dozen seconds of being a gooey mess in his arms.*

The role of fate that day was never lost on me. Like had Chase thought it was his job to look out for me while my brothers hiked and canoed around a lake in the Blue Ridge mountains? Why *had* he come over to clean the horse stalls while they were away? Could he have secretly liked me as much as I liked him…?

I muffled a laugh. *Evidence clearly points to no.*

A breeze brushed over my shoulders, stirring more memories of Chase. I pictured a tall, husky adolescent Chase filling out his polo and khaki shorts. Clearly, awkward limbs and runaway acne hadn't existed in the Bova gene pool because he was all tight muscle and smooth jaws. When he wasn't tied down with afternoon soccer practice, he'd go fishing on the lake in his boat, and judging by social media, he spent his weekends with the prettiest girls in Vista Falls.

He and Thorne ran with the same crowd throughout high school, but when it came time for college, Chase skipped out for a summer job on a shrimp boat near Charleston, South Carolina. Soon after, he started his own channel and began filming kayaking trips along the rivers in North and South Carolina. Then, more fishing, more filming, more followers, until one day, Chase n' Dreams was a reality.

All I knew was in the end, Chase Bova left home for greener pastures—or rather bluer waters—and took my crush with him.

"Hey, Prim," Thorne said, flicking his head toward the oak tree. "You remember the treehouse Chase and I built that summer?"

I nodded quickly, tucking a strand of hair behind my ear.

"Too bad we had to tear it down when the wood began to rot." He raised the lid on the grill, reached for the platter, and began filling it with food. "I should've taken you up there, you know. At least once. It was stupid to keep it off limits." He gave me his can't-forget-you smile again. "I'm kind of sorry you missed it."

A rush tingled over my skin only there was no breeze in the air. *Guess Chase didn't tell you after all.*

Elbows on the table, I tucked my hands beneath my chin and lifted my face toward the sky. The familiar backyard scents of freshly mowed grass and gardenias filled my nostrils. I wiggled my butt on the same patio chair that'd been at this table my whole life. *Don't be sorry, Thorne. I'm glad you barred me from The Hideout.*

Otherwise I never would've snuck up the tree the moment you left for camp.

And then Chase would've never caught me.

And I would've missed those brief moments where I felt safe with him.

While I'd never forgotten that day—and I'd kept tabs on Chase through his social media accounts—he didn't cloud my thoughts so much anymore.

Until today.

I rubbed my hand over the stubborn lump forming in my throat. It was, after all, just a crush and by definition was fleeting and totally without reason.

I steadied my breath and gave Thorne my best grin. "Hey, don't worry about it."

With a nod, he turned off the gas grill, grabbed the platter, and asked me to bring the cooler to the table. He settled into the chair across from me, interrupting the silence when he said, "Are you doing all right, Prim?"

Only he or my younger sister, Goldie, would ask me that question, because while I loved all my brothers and sisters, I was closest to them. I moved in my seat, hedging. "Better I think. Throwing myself into work helps."

"You work too damn much," Thorne grumbled.

I swatted him on the arm. "I like work. And I'm a damn good nurse."

"I wish you'd tell me what that douchebag lawyer, Aimless, did to you."

"Avery." I corrected and added, "Why, so you can meddle in my business?"

"Caring and meddling are two completely different things." At my arched eyebrow, he paused then added more quietly, "Okay, so maybe I'm protective."

"Just a little."

"I only want the best for you. To see you out there mingling with people, socializing, enjoying life."

"You're confusing me with Goldie. She mingles and charms the room. I examine and diagnose it."

His tone cooled. "Are you ever going to tell me what really went down with Ass Wipe?"

I paused, my beer partway to my lips, then lowered it to the table. "I told you everything you need to know. Avery and I were just too different. We were never going to last, so I broke it off."

Thorne tipped his head back and pulled on his beer. "He hurt you, which makes me want to strangle him."

"Yeah, but I'm moving on. Really."

"Are you dating anyone?"

I tilted my head to one side and extended my hand. "Ah, hello, Pot. I'm Kettle. Have we met?"

Thorne laughed, a rich sound deep in his gut, and it drew me in, as always.

I had to laugh with him…at least a little. "And how's the dating game going for *you* these days?"

After regaining his composure, he wagged his finger at me. "This conversation isn't about me. Besides, I'm not interested in dating when I'll be leaving soon."

I hated the reminder his stay in Vista Falls was temporary. He'd only come home to oversee the restoration of Old Rambler, our farm's original house and barn, and a series of cottages. "When do you have to be back in Atlanta?"

As Thorne pondered my question, thoughts colored his expression. My brother was an attorney, and while he maintained his license in Georgia, he no longer actively practiced law. And that was a blessing—one none of us saw coming.

Our parents taught us to look for the good when something bad happened. I didn't think this logic always worked—like I hadn't uncovered any good out of my toxic relationship with Avery—but the sentiment held true on one account when our father died of heart disease before his fiftieth birthday.

Out of the three Vreeland sons, Thorne was our dad's clone. Both men were six foot two and broad shouldered, prone to mask their worries behind a joke or a laugh. Though they worked in vastly different occupations, they approached farming and law at similar speeds. *Full throttle.*

We were all shocked by Dad's death, but Thorne processed his grief in a very personal way. He found running again, dropping thirty pounds in the first year, but more importantly, he ditched the courtroom grind and exhausting trek to partnership. He chose to stay in the greater Atlanta area, dusting off his undergraduate degree in architectural history and accepting a part time adjunct faculty position at a nearby private college.

With convenient access to the city's Interstate highways and international airport, Thorne got busy teaching and building his credentials as a historic preservation consultant. He assisted with the restoration of the chapel on the college's campus, and after getting a few more projects under his belt, was elected to the board of a regional historical preservation society. These days, my brother traveled the East Coast, leaving his signature on architectural landmarks and finding joy in teaching.

I gazed at Thorne from across the table, taking in his nicely tanned skin and thick blond hair tied back in a messy ponytail. He no longer had a crease imprinted on his brow, and he'd finally stopped chewing his fingernails and bouncing his knee. He could still tell a really good joke, only now he laughed along with us at the punchline.

Yeah, I think Dad saved Thorne. And that was the only good any of us could find in his untimely death.

"Actually, classes don't begin until after Labor Day," Thorne said, pulling my thoughts to the present. "Before I head back, I'm thinking about going to Savannah."

I lifted a brow and tried to sound casual. "Are you talking about the city of Savannah...or Savannah, your friend from law school?"

"Don't try to change the subject. This conversation is about you, remember?" My brother winked, and I sighed, blowing a wisp of hair off my cheek. "I know you don't believe me." He pointed at me with his beer. "But you could have a guy in your life again if you wanted it."

I wiped a sweat bead up the side of my bottle and flicked the droplet off my finger. "I wish it was that easy."

As our matching, blue-eyed gazes met, I proceeded

to describe the plight of women my age. I enlightened him to our battles of trying to dress sexy without looking too young and slutty. I explained dating meant checking an app on my phone for matches multiple times a day, something incredibly hard to do in a trauma room. Plowing through a feed of likes from guys, wondering if the next one to appear on my screen might actually be Mr. Right, exhausted me. And when it came to the first meetup?

"Do you know what a letdown it is when a guy asks you out on a Wednesday or Thursday night?" Thorne shook his head, bewildered. "He's saying I'm not worth a coveted weekend slot."

"But you're a nurse. You work some weekends. Maybe the guy's just being considerate."

"No. It doesn't work that way."

My brother rolled his eyes. "I can tell you this. Guys don't think about any of that shit. At least I don't."

"Well, maybe you should."

Thorne plunked his bottle on the table. "Maybe you should call somebody."

I stared at him, mouth open. "*Somebody*? Who'd you have in mind?" I perked up in my chair. "I've lived in Raleigh for the last eight years. I suck at relationships. I work too much. I'm kinda fresh out of 'somebodies,' don't you think?"

Thorne quieted me with a look. "I'm not telling you what to—"

"Yeah, you kinda are." It was my turn to roll my eyes.

"Just, you know…call a friend. Call *somebody*." He sighed, turning his head as if the answer to my pathetic love life was hidden behind the azalea blooms bordering the patio. As I swatted at a dragonfly zipping past my head, Thorne snapped his fingers. He swung his gaze my way and flashed me his can't-forget-you smile. "What about Chase?"

My mouth opened, but no words came out. Even though the perfect retort was right there on the edge of my tongue, I couldn't produce a single sound.

"I mean, you know him. He's a good guy. I'm sure he wouldn't mind getting out some now he's back home." Thorne tipped his head back, polishing off his beer. "Shit, you're my sister, so he'd never get out of line or anything."

Have you lost your mind?

Suddenly, the screen door squeaked, and Mom and Ace came out carrying the salad and sweet tea. They joined us at the table, and after Ace blessed the food, we began filling our plates.

While spreading butter on her ear of corn, Mom said, "Ace and I were just talking. What d'you think about having Chase over for supper one night?"

My hand jerked, and my knife slid down the chicken breast, scratching across my plate.

Mom turned her head in my direction.

Ace arched his eyebrows at me.

But Thorne simply tossed a cherry tomato into his mouth. "Great idea. He's just the *somebody* we need, right, Prim?" He grinned as he chewed, clearly ignoring their puzzled looks and my blank expression. "He'll be at Brent and Tiffany's wedding on Saturday. I'll ask him then."

Flip an effing blueberry pancake!

Suddenly, singing one song for the happy couple wasn't a problem. It was full-scale pandemonium whirling through my stomach. *Chase will be at the wedding reception...where he'll hear me sing a song I've never practiced...and then sit down with us for supper sometime soon...?*

I poured a glass of sweet tea and brought it to my lips, attempting to drown my freak-out with a long swallow. I took another sip. And then another. I lowered my glass on the tabletop with a quiet thump.

Nope. That didn't help. Not even a little bit...

Chapter Two

Saturday, August 6th 6:50 p.m.
Chase

There was never anything small about a small-town wedding. Though the bride had only lived in Vista Falls for a few years, the groom was from here. Brent Conard was a police officer and one of a dozen volunteer high school football coaches, so there wasn't an empty seat in the church.

After the ceremony, everyone made their way over to Old Rambler at Three Creeks Farm for the reception. My best friend, Thorne Vreeland, had recently moved home to oversee the renovations to his family's original farmhouse and barn. He'd transformed the house into a boutique bed-and-breakfast with a string of quaint villas. As my gaze traveled around the old barn turned event venue, his commitment to preserving the charm and historic elements of the place shone through. With hundreds of lights flickering overhead, masses of flowers in pots and displays, band playing and guests dancing on rustic hardwood flooring, I gave Thorne a mental high five.

"Whatha thinkin' 'bout, Unca Thase?" Charlotte asked around an enormous mouthful of wedding cake. My niece gazed at me with her curious brown eyes, and my heart softened. She was a living, breathing reminder of what I'd always believed about life. *Collect memories, not things.*

I reached for a napkin, and she lifted her chin for me to wipe it across her mouth. I cocked my head, smiling. "Oh, I dunno. Maybe thinking about how beautiful you're going to look at your wedding someday."

Charlotte took a sip of punch, then a tiny crease formed across her forehead. "But Miss Tiffany's daddy walked her into the church. I don't have a daddy anymore."

My sister, Carrie, had been married for six years when an undiagnosed heart condition claimed her husband's life. Afterward, she and Charlotte moved home to be near friends and Grandpa. The frown on my niece's face reminded me of life's cruelty.

I leaned forward and kissed the top of her head. "You have me, Kitten. I'll walk you down the aisle. I'll be here for you, for all the important things in your life. Promise."

"I'm glad you're here, Uncle Chase. Will you teach me how to fish? I *am* four years old now."

Seamlessly, Charlotte hopped on to the next thought in her head. Thank God, children were resilient, able to move forward from tragedy like ants marching to a picnic. *Me and Carrie included.*

I spoke over a chuckle, meeting her questioning gaze. "I'd like to take you fishing. But we'll need to get your mom's okay first."

"She'll say yes. I know she will. She all the time says she wants you to be happy." Charlotte swiped her finger through a dollop of icing left on her plate and popped it in her mouth, licking it clean. "Fishing makes you happy, so fishing with me would be the most happy!"

"Hey, you two." Carrie stepped between us, placing a hand on each of our shoulders. "By the look of your face, I'd say you enjoyed your piece of cake." She licked her thumb and rubbed it over a spot I missed on Charlotte's cheek.

"I ate *two*, Mommy."

"Two slices of cake?" Carrie turned to me. "Is that so...?"

"Hey, I'd like to see you say no to those big brown eyes," I said, holding up my hands.

Carrie whispered something about me being a complete pushover, then playfully swatted my arm. She took the seat beside me, then leaned in close, giving me the run down on every unattached female in the room. I loosened the knot in my tie and settled in for the show. When I quirked an eyebrow at the curvy, middle-aged woman she'd skipped over in her narrative, Carrie shook her head.

"You best ignore that one with the snakeskin belt. That's Tiffany's aunt from Amarillo. She told me she's a bit of a lush and a real cougar, always looking for a good time."

"Just my type."

Carrie swatted me again, only this time a little harder, and I laughed. "I'm kidding, okay? Not into cougars, but I do like a good time."

She hummed and nodded as only a big sister can. The band switched to an upbeat dance song, but the air between us quieted.

"Okay, out with it," I said.

Carrie crossed her arms on the table. "I'm just

thinking about your type of woman. She has to fit your schedule, your calendar, your current location. No strings, no attachments."

I drew my eyebrows down. "And what d'you know about the women I spend time with?"

"Sadly, very little. Because you never tell me anything." She waved her fingers in my direction. "And I can count on one hand how many times you've been home in the last ten years."

I reached for my drink, the whiskey burning a trail down my throat.

"But I've seen pictures online. 'Chase n' Dreams' is more than hooking a fish on your line. You're like a kernel in hot oil, popping up with a different girl in every town. A damn sailor...only with a kayak, a helmet camera, and a fishing rod."

"Don't forget my endorsements. And all of those followers and subscribers. I can't help it if women proposition me." I chuckled, but her frown only deepened.

In school, I was that kid who when hammered with a list of his shortcomings, heaped on a few more for good measure. If Carrie was going all deep-shit personal on me, the least I could do was help her out.

"That's exactly what I'm talking about." She finger-pointed in my direction. "I hope you've ditched the river groupies for good and are ready to get back to your Carolina roots. Finding love means spending more than a couple of weeks in a time zone. Start dating, find someone you can get close to."

"Not my style, Carrie. You know that."

"But you've got such a huge heart." She reached for my plate and forked a bite of cake in her mouth. "I guess

I just don't understand why you keep it locked up. I mean, aren't you ready to meet a woman who knocks you on your ass? Who hugs your heart and steals your breath and gets inside your head so bad you can't think straight?"

I spoke over the rim of my glass. "Name one man who wants to feel like that."

Carrie's gaze skated over to Charlotte and then back to me. "Lucas."

I covered my eyes with my hand and sighed. Leave it to me to forget how in love Carrie and her husband were, and how they made such an amazing little girl. *Fuck.* "I'm sorry, Carrie. I wasn't thinking."

My sister grabbed my hand and squeezed it. "You said exactly what I knew you'd say. You like being in control, and well, love pretty much turns your life upside down. God gave me an amazing gift, and Lucas and I loved each other for as long as we could. I just want you to find that kind of happiness, that kind of love, too."

Carrie had a way of plowing through the bullshit and getting real. But I wasn't a kid anymore, and even though I knew this was all coming from a place of love, irritation clawed my gut.

"I'm home, aren't I? Isn't that enough for now?" I dug my fingers under my collar, desperate to put some air between it and my skin. "Did you ever think I might have my reasons for wanting some down time?"

"Maybe. But again, how would I know?" She leaned in closer and touched my arm. "Hey, just get it through your sunbaked fish brain I'm still your big sister…and a damn good listener. Whatever you need, okay?"

Our gazes met for a few moments, then I squeezed her hand. I thought about when we were kids, and how

Mom moved us in with Grandpa when our dad left us. Since Curt Bova, our stock-car-mechanic-turned-gambling-addict father, wasn't around to dole out affection, Mom had made sure to drown us in hers. And I'd shared mine right back, freely giving her all my best hugs and kisses.

But everything changed when Mom got cancer. I was only seven years old, but some things about that time were etched in my memory. Like the smell of Grandpa's corned beef and cabbage cooking on the stove. And the weight of Carrie's arm over my shoulder when she walked me to my soccer games. And the click of the hospital bed being closed and rolled out of the house the day after Mom died.

After we laid her to rest in the grave beside my grandmother, my heart shrank a couple of sizes. I saved what little was left of it for Carrie, Grandpa, and my best friend, Thorne. At least until Charlotte came along. Somehow, that little kitten had snuck her way into my heart while I wasn't looking. But even now, as a thirty-four-year-old river dog, I kept my heart locked up in a black trunk. I was pretty sure if I ever found a special someone and gave it to her, she'd snap it clean in two.

I released my sister's hand. It was so like her to believe there was a perfect match out there for me, as if slowing down my life would make this woman magically appear. Carrie had found love with Lucas, but then she'd always liked who she was. She was lovable. *Me...? Not so much, no.*

In truth, I was too much like my father to be loved. We were both restless, selfish, single-minded...and womanizing. But that was where the similarities ended. In no way did I share his weakness for gambling and alcohol.

While I hadn't seen Curt in a dozen years, a private investigator kept me informed of his whereabouts, most recently near Concord, North Carolina. Seemed his addictions forced him off his race car team and into a ton of debt. Where Curt was concerned, I'd adopted the "keep your enemies closer" philosophy and slept better with updates on his comings and goings.

I felt a tug on my jacket and gazed down at the littlest love of my life. "Will you dance with me, Uncle Chase?"

Grateful for the interruption to my thoughts, I gave Carrie a quiet smile and led Charlotte to the dance floor. We swayed from side to side and when I twirled her around, her blonde hair fanned around her shoulders. Her hands were small inside mine, and she gazed at me with so much trust it made my chest hurt.

As the song came to an end, I lifted Charlotte in my arms and stepped aside to make way for the bridal couple. The band shifted into a slow ballad, and everyone watched as Brent pulled Tiffany close for their first dance as husband and wife.

I turned toward the band the instant I heard the new vocalist. Familiarity made my neck warm. The woman's soft voice filled the air, and after several beats, my mind slipped away to a simpler time.

Saturdays…chores in the morning then soccer or fishing in the afternoon.

Me and Thorne escaping to the treehouse Hideout with our survival food—a sack of trail mix and a case of root beer.

And Thorne's little sister singing away while she pumped back and forth on the tire swing.

I gazed at the singer on stage, toes peeking out of strappy high heel sandals. *No more seriously worn-out sneakers.* A smile twitched my lips. *And while this dress is sexy as hell, I can't forget how cute you looked in those cutoff jean shorts.*

I lowered Charlotte to her feet and watched her skip over to Carrie before turning my full attention to the stage. Other guests had joined the bride and groom on the dance floor, but I couldn't drag my gaze from *her*. I crossed my arms over my chest, full-on smiling now.

Damn. Primrose Vreeland.

I stilled, memories I didn't know I had creeping over me. Like when Prim was eight and I caught her climbing down from The Hideout, I saved her from falling to the ground. Even though she was a few years behind me in school, I found her name on a list of chemistry tutors my advisor suggested I contact during *my* senior year. *Only I never did.*

As we got older, it seemed like every time I hung out with Thorne, she was babysitting her younger siblings or digging around in her mom's vegetable garden. *And looking really cute with a bandana tied around her ponytail.* And during swim season, I spotted her picture in the newspaper a few times. *Because get real, athletes always pay attention to other athletes.*

I lowered my head as the reasons I'd steered clear of Prim in high school slowly came into focus.

For one thing, I was the typical cocky eighteen-year-old, totally self-absorbed and looking to get laid as easily and often as possible. Then there was the fact she was Thorne's kid sister, and I wasn't into racking up frequent flyer miles with virgins. I scrubbed my knuckles across my jaw. *Bull fucking shit.* It was mostly because she was

Primrose, as beautiful and innocent as the wildflower she was named after, and I was more of a...cactus.

As she launched into the chorus one last time, she closed her eyes and held a high note so perfectly I found it hard to breathe...to think...to remember my own fucking name.

As her voice trailed away, I blinked into awareness. Then Prim opened her blue eyes and stared straight into mine.

****

Prim

"Hey everybody, how about we show a little love to Prim for singing the couple's first song?"

My head snapped up and toward the sound of my name from the band's lead singer. With applause lifting in the air, I dragged my gaze from Chase Bova long enough to blow a kiss to Tiffany and thank the band. I stepped off stage and skirted around the edge of the dance floor. I tried to ignore the pressure of his gaze and focused on not tripping in my three-inch heels.

"Prim!"

I stopped and turned around...and sucked in a breath. As good as Chase looked in his videos, the camera fell short of capturing his simmering, rugged good looks. He was even taller than I remembered, and his chest and shoulders still qualified for their own zip code. His hair was thick and sandy blond, a little mussed, but smoothed back with the ends brushing his neck. His biceps looked as though they could bench press a cow without so much as a flinch.

His warm, lazy smile lent a hint of mischief to his face. His approach was interrupted by a couple of guys wanting to shake his hand, and when he turned his head toward them, I glimpsed the hard line of his jaw and smooth neck.

When he got to me, his expression softened like he was looking at someone familiar yet seeing her altogether differently. *Or maybe it's just my wishful thinking.*

"Hey."

I steadied my breath before speaking. "Hi."

He tipped his head toward the stage. "Wow, that right there? That was nothing like how you sang when you were a kid." I must have pulled a puzzled look because he quickly added, "You know, your tire swing serenades?"

I bit my lower lip, fighting a smile. "Oh, God. You remember that…?"

"I do. I heard you loud and clear in The Hideout. Kind of drove Thorne a little crazy sometimes, but I dunno," he said, shrugging. "It never bothered me so much."

I took a step forward and threw my arms around him. Not at all what I'd planned in anticipation of seeing him again, but it felt right. Being so close to him made me feel like I was a kid again. Only brushing against his chest reminded me, well…he was no kid.

Chase whispered over my ear. "It's good to see you."

I nodded, knowing I should let him go, but he smelled too good—like mint and clean soap. When I finally released him, I said quietly, "It's good to see you, too."

He stepped backward, looking me over, the corners of his mouth turning up. "You look different."

Shit, that's a loaded word. I tilted my head, tucking

a lock of hair behind my ear. "Well, it's pretty amazing what braces and a curling iron can do for a girl."

Eyes the color of tobacco stared into mine. Slowly, his gaze drifted to my mouth and then up to my eyes. The air between us hummed with energy, but...*no*. I was totally misreading the moment and the man.

"So," I said, stretching out the word.

Chase blinked, as if coming back from some deep thought. "So. Right." He coughed lightly. "Thorne told me you just moved home. How do you like working at the hospital here?"

A server came by carrying a tray, and Chase grabbed two glasses of champagne. He handed one to me and waited for me to take the first sip.

"Well, the people are great." I glanced around the room at folks we'd both known for most our lives. "I love the staff. They're some of the best I've ever worked with."

He nodded. "Nothing better than being happy at work. Makes all the difference."

"Says the world-traveling fisherman and social media influencer."

He shrugged. "It's not like my face is on a cereal box."

"No, but it gets a shit ton of likes."

My retort got a tug from his lips, and he leaned toward me. "Have you watched me, Prim...?"

The timbre of his voice did funny things to my insides, sending my good sense skidding into a ravine. I tilted my head, grinning. "Maybe."

As his expression brightened, I felt myself slipping under his spell. *This is how he pulls in all those followers.*

I sipped my champagne, then peeked up at him. "Okay, yes, just a couple of times. But don't let it go to your head or anything."

"Do you have a favorite video?"

Uh, hello? All of them...because you're in *all of them.* But that wasn't what I said. "I liked the one where you were catching and cooking rainbow trout at Lake Michigan—with the group of middle schoolers."

He rubbed the back of his knuckles over his lip. "Yeah. That one was very cool. Most of those kids had never touched a fishing rod."

I paused with the champagne glass in my hand, intrigued. "How'd you come up with the idea?"

"I got an email from a boy in this group home in Green Bay—said he and his friends were big fans. Of course, I sent them a dozen photographs signed by me and the crew, and some sweatshirts from the online apparel shop." His brown eyes softened before he continued. "But I wanted to do more, you know? So, I learned all I could about the home, gave their director a call, and had the show sketched out in a week."

"You know you made their day—giving them that experience with a famous *adventurer*."

He took a slow breath and dragged his hand over his neck. "Sorry, but I don't think of myself like that. I've been lucky to be able to do something I love and make a living out of it. I try to pay it forward when I can. I'm really not much different from the next guy—"

I watched as Chase tilted his head back and drained his champagne.

"—or you, *Nurse* Vreeland."

I gazed at the smile starting on one side of his mouth and followed it until it slid into place. His gentle manner drew me in, and without thinking I offered, "You know, I think I like being a nurse here more than Raleigh. I know it might sound crazy, but our regional hospital gives me more one-on-one time with my patients. It's more personal."

He touched my arm, making my skin tingle. "You save lives, Prim. Every day. Few people can say that about their work. I think you're the famous one—to your patients and their families. To pretty much anyone who knows you."

And this is how Chase Bova charms the women. I glanced past him, spotting my brother approaching from three o'clock. *Just in time.*

Chase stepped toward me. "Hey, I was thinking maybe we—"

"Hey, buddy!" Thorne said, throwing an arm around Chase. "I've been looking for you."

They embraced, then fell into an easy conversation. Seeing them together was like rewinding time, only their voices were deeper and their hair longer. I was just about to slip away—because I didn't want to stick around for Thorne to hogtie Chase into being my *somebody*—when my brother turned my way.

"And did you hear Prim sing? Man, wasn't she something?"

Chase cocked his head, considering me for a heartbeat. Something about the way his gaze lingered over me made me want to stand taller, to be seen. "Yeah. She's great. Really great."

Thorne thumped Chase on the arm. "Come with me. We've got Brent's car parked out back. Gotta cover it with shaving cream and tin cans before they head out."

Chase laughed, the deep sound of it filling the air

between us. He started to follow my brother, then paused and turned to me. "This won't take long. If it's okay with you, maybe we can sit and talk a little more when I get back."

I nodded, a little too quickly, because I knew how this ended. With me getting lost in my crush, thinking he might be my *somebody*.

Or worse, had Thorne already talked to him, and now I was his charity case?

Oh, hell no.

I smiled quietly and managed a little white lie. "Sure, Chase."

Chapter Three

Monday, August 8th 7:05 p.m.
Chase

I stood in front of the mirror in the men's locker room, hands on the waist of my jogging pants, and stared at my reflection. *Swimming really sucks.* If God meant for humans to move through the water—outside of a boat or kayak—he'd have given us gills instead of lungs. I shook my head. *Everybody knows fat floats and muscle sinks.* Which meant my body was an anchor in the water. Nevertheless, I couldn't hide from the truth. Swimming burned calories and was easy on my joints. *Freestyle is my new best friend.*

I ran a comb through my hair, pulled on a Chase n' Dreams T-shirt, and shrugged my duffle bag over one shoulder. As I stepped outside the hospital fitness center, I thumbed through my texts, landing on a selfie from Carrie and Charlotte. They were holding cupcakes, wearing matching aprons and flour speckles on their cheeks. I chuckled at the caption and string of smiley-heart emojis with the message, *Look what we made!* I slapped my hand on my stomach. The scales in the gym didn't lie—I'd added two pounds since moving home. While I texted my sister a thumbs-up, I swore—unlike the dozen or so brownies I devoured last week—I'd only eat one cupcake.

I climbed into my truck, started the engine, and pressed the button for seat heat. I reached for my water bottle, fighting a dryness in my throat that seemed to appear every time I thought about my family and what had brought me back home. Carrie laid into me pretty good at the wedding reception, and though it'd felt shitty at the time, I needed the reminder my roots were here. *I hope I can salvage them despite my years of neglect.*

"I don't give a shit it's August," I said to the empty cab of my truck, shifting my hips so the seat heat pressed right on my tailbone. "That feels damn good."

I stared out the window at the clouds tipped in shades of purple and orange. The sun would be setting soon. *End of another day.*

End of another day without Chase n' Dreams...

Stepping away from the business I'd started fourteen years ago had shaken me, but the unease wasn't about money. I had healthy bank accounts, several rental properties, and sizable annuities in place for both Carrie and Charlotte. I hadn't needed an economics degree to figure out recession-resistant business investments made sense.

Part of the success of Chase n' Dreams stemmed from my instincts. I was good at ferreting out money opportunities from money pits—and even better at doing it with people. Those skills had served me well in negotiating the sale of my shares and securing my new position as executive producer and creative consultant. I could do the job either on location or remotely from home.

I looked out my windshield and sighed, realizing bald fear lurked in the pit of my stomach. Fishing had been my high, my focus my whole life. Fishing had never failed me. But my body had sure as hell failed fishing.

While I wasn't ready to be put out to pasture, my achy joints were a liability to the team. I'd chalked it up to life on the road—hours spent filming trips on the water, partying with friends, and sleeping on a pullout bed in the camper. There was no denying arthritis ran in my mother's family. *And as for Curt Bova?* God only knew what slithered through his DNA.

"Shit." I slammed the steering wheel with my hand. While my brain wrestled with the crapshoot of aging and genetics, something bigger twisted in my gut.

Prim Vreeland stood me up.

I'd tried like hell the past two days to figure out why this bugged me so much. Like Carrie said, women had to fit my schedule, calendar, and location…not the other way around. My hookups shared my lust for adventure. I liked the sexy outdoorsy type—often models or media reps for one of my sponsors—who avoided attachment same as me. That kind of woman never left me guessing, never gave me the slip when my back was turned. But Prim had, and I didn't like it one damn bit.

I rolled down the window, reversed out of my parking space, and drove through the hospital employee lot. I braked at the stop sign and turned my head toward the setting sun.

"What the—?" a voice cried, followed by a whale-like moan. "Flip an ever-loving pancake!"

I whipped around to get a better look and spotted a woman crouched at her front right tire. *This is priceless.* I pulled into the first available spot, killed the engine, and walked over to the damsel in distress with a skip in my step.

I cleared my throat with a pointed cough. "Is there a problem, Prim?"

She jumped up. "Chase!" She grabbed her throat, shrieking so loudly I stepped backward. "You scared the shit out of me."

"Jesus. Sorry." I scrubbed my hand across the back of my neck. "I was just trying to help." No, I wasn't. I was gloating.

But now I really want to help.

As she regained her breath, she muttered, "Thanks, but it's okay. I'll just call the Auto Connection guys."

I watched her fish her phone out of her bag. Her thumbs skimmed over the screen, and as caveman as it sounds, I didn't like being tossed aside like moldy bread.

I stepped forward, closing my hand over her fingers. "I can change a flat tire."

She lifted her chin. "I can, too." But then her shoulders sank a couple inches, and she sighed. "I-I just don't feel like doing it right now."

I studied the way the wind ruffled her blue cotton dress and how her toes fit perfectly inside her cushiony flip-flops. She looked comfortable. Her limbs undoubtedly grateful for the space after being trapped in a uniform all day. *I can relate. Hours in a kayak are a literal pain in the ass.* Her blonde hair was in one long braid down her back, short wisps of hair clinging to her nape. *I know something about perspiration-flushed cheeks, too.* The part of me hung up on her ditching me Saturday night was silenced by my protective side.

I wanted to help her out of a jam. "Long day in emergency, huh?"

Prim nodded and dropped her phone in her bag. Her lips formed a thin line, then the bottom one began to quiver.

Shit. My eyes narrowed. "Was it worse? Was it a *bad* day?"

She met my gaze, sniffing.

Damn. Without thinking, I closed the space between us and wrapped her in my arms. Like at the wedding, she felt good pressed against me, as if she somehow belonged there. She trembled as she buried her face in my chest. I rubbed my hands in circles over her back until she went still. I didn't know what to say, so I did what Grandpa taught me to do with emotional females. *Keep my damn mouth shut.*

Prim leaned back, dabbing her eyes with her fingers and pointing. "I got mascara on your shirt. Now your logo says, 'Chase Ho Dreams.' "

I glanced down and sure enough, the *n* had turned into the word "ho." I chuckled. "You know, you're right. Sounds like a name for a reality TV show. Like chasing Santa in your dreams—ho, ho, ho."

She cracked a smile. "Or 'Chase Ho Dreams,' like one of those dating shows where the hot guy goes chasing after a ho?" She quickly sucked in a breath. "I meant woman. Shit. You know what I mean."

I threw my head back and laughed. "That's pretty good. You know, I don't think I'm going to wash this." I gazed down at the smeared letter, then up at Prim. "I'll post about it tomorrow. The RugRog crowd will love it." Her face paled, and I quickly added, "But I won't say anything about you or how it happened."

"No, I mean I know you wouldn't. I was just thinking about how crazy it is you're famous. I never think about posting, but then there's no one following me."

"I know, it's shallow."

She scrunched her nose. "Maybe just a little."

I raised my finger in explanation. "But it boosts ratings and attracts more sponsors, which in turn is good for business."

She raised the corners of her lips. "Got to love those endorsements."

I bent my knees so I could meet her eye level. "Please tell me I'm not borderline narcissistic."

"Okay. I'm not borderline narcissistic," she said, snorting around the last word.

That's got to be the cutest damn sound I've ever heard.

A grin teased her lips, and I cracked a smile. Then we both broke out in laughter, and maybe a little too late, I realized my hands had fallen to her waist. I slowly eased back, arms by my sides.

"Are you really going to post this?" Prim pointed at the logo on my shirt then placed her palm over her collarbone. "I mean, I understand if you have to."

My gaze fell to her hand. It was small, and her cuticles were smooth, nails unpolished. She had healing hands, giving hands. Hands I imagined would feel amazing on my—

I dragged my hand over my jaw. "Nah, I was just fooling around, and I don't want to share that with anyone but you." I lifted my gaze to hers. "But just so you know, I'm never washing this."

Relief shone in her eyes, and she giggled. "And what're you gonna do with it?"

Several dirty ideas popped into my head, but none I dared share with Prim. I liked her, and I wanted her to like me, too. So keeping my thoughts to myself, I switched gears, knowing sometimes catching the right fish meant switching your bait.

"Give it to you, of course. So you can hold on to it the next time you're sad. Maybe it'll make you feel better."

"Kinda like a security blanket?"

"Yeah."

"I'd like that." She gifted me a smile. "Thank you, Chase."

My name coming from her lips sounded like yesterday and forever wrapped up in one. I wanted to keep her with me, feel the warmth of her gaze for as long as possible.

I pointed to the blaze of russet orange above the pine trees. "Hey, d'you see that sun over there?" She nodded. "If you'll just kick back in the bed of my truck for about ten minutes, you can watch it set while I change your tire."

"But—"

"Open the trunk, please." I had patience galore, but it only took a handful of seconds for her to follow my command. I glanced inside the pair of cube organizers in her trunk, spotting a first aid kit—*naturally*—and a carton of protein bars, some bottled waters, and a canister of sanitizing wipes. I swallowed a smile as I grabbed the spare tire and toolkit.

"Chase—"

"Trust me. I know what I'm talking about. Sunsets are beautiful and relaxing."

"You really don't have to do this."

I closed the trunk and turned around, studying how she stood, weight on her right side, hand on her hip. I set the tire and tools on the ground and raked my hand through my hair. For as much as I knew Prim—my best friend's dorky little chemistry-loving, songbird sister—I was finding I didn't know her at all. I'd never made any apologies for my appreciation of the fairer sex, and there was little I hadn't done with them, to them, or for them. But this woman…?

She knocks me on my ass.

The memory of Carrie's words rattled me. I'd been careful to avoid Prim all those years ago. But now…?

Yeah, it's about damn time I cast my line for Prim Vreeland.

"I know I don't have to fix your flat. But the thing is I want to." I crossed my arms over my chest. "And after I fix your flat, we're going to the Sundae Hut for a milkshake. It's the best for curing long, bad days. That, and well, sunsets."

A smile reached her eyes, and I liked thinking I had something to do with it.

I took her hand in mine and led her to my truck. "And then we're going to sit and talk awhile. But you'll have to ride with me since I can't be sure you'll actually follow me there," I said with a wink. "I'm not going to give you the chance to ditch me again."

****

Prim

In the end, I wasn't sure which gave me more comfort—watching the sunset or having Chase take care of me. I was pretty adept at life on my own, not used to having a man's no-strings-attached help. Although if I was honest, any strings connecting Chase and me would have been more of a dream than a concern.

True to his word, Chase drove us to the Sundae Hut, led me inside, and ordered us a couple of milkshakes and a basket of fries. He didn't seem to notice how the teenage girl, with her lip wedged between her teeth, stood behind the register staring at his chest. He also missed her breathy sigh when he stuffed several bills in the tip jar.

The teenager's harmless flirtation made me gaze down at my outfit. Hospital employees turned in their scrubs after every shift, and while a cotton sundress might feel like heaven after a long day, this one wasn't the least bit sexy. And another thing that wasn't sexy? *Crying on Chase after losing a patient in cardiac arrest.* Something about Chase made me turn all gushy and mushy—it'd been like that my whole life. This evening was just another convenient rescue—not so different from the tree house freefall—and reminded me of what a dorky kid I'd been. *And now I'm a quirky woman.*

"This place hasn't changed a bit," Chase said, toying with the paper ticket number in his hand. A grin spread across his full lips, the dimple on his right cheek deepening before he led us across the dining room. He paused to shake hands with a few people along the way, then waited while I scooted inside the booth before he took his place across from me.

He dropped the ticket on the mint green laminate tabletop and intertwined his fingers in a single fist, his movements steady and deliberate. His hands bore some scars, but overall his skin was smooth, weathered but not worn out. As I imagined his hands wrapped around a fishing rod, miles of powerful legs hidden inside a kayak, my pulse quickened.

Chase pulled some napkins from the tabletop dispenser and stacked them between us. He lowered his voice, looking around. "Something tells me there are no loyalty points for ordering on an app either."

I smiled, shifting in my seat and scrunching my toes in my flip-flops. "True. But you get a free hot fudge sundae on your birthday."

Chase quietly chuckled. "How could I forget?" His eyes narrowed. "So, when's yours?"

My heart skipped a beat. "My birthday?" He nodded. "Um, June."

He sat up a little taller. "June…?"

"Sixteenth," I said quietly. "And yours is June twenty-second."

"How'd you—?"

Our order number ringing over the intercom cut him off, then he slid out of the booth. Elbows on the table, I pressed my face in my hands, my gaze tracking the movement of his muscular thighs and tight ass. His T-shirt stretched over his back with just enough tightness to showcase his muscles. The waistband of his joggers rested low on his hips, the lines of his thighs visible beneath the performance fabric. I ran my tongue across my bottom lip, catching myself before I drooled.

Chase returned with our food, and as we munched on fries and sipped our milkshakes, my teeth tingled. Only the sensation had little to do with ice cream…and everything to do with *him*.

Him, with his sparkling brown eyes and sexy dimple.

Him, with no sign of a receding, thinning hairline.

Him, with his straight teeth that never needed braces.

"What are you thinking, Prim?"

I lowered my glass to the table and ran a fry through the mound of ketchup on my plate. I shrugged. "Just about how men age so much better than women. You've got great hair."

He chuckled. "Glad you like it. If I'm anything like my grandpa, the blond will be silver by the time I'm fifty." He stirred his milkshake with his straw and took a long sip. "So…I'm curious how you knew my birthday."

I crossed my hands on the tabletop. "I just always remember it being a week after mine. Plus, you guys built the treehouse the summer you turned eleven. I still remember Mom stopping Thorne and taking the birthday candles off the cupcakes so you two wouldn't burn down the backyard."

Chase laughed and rubbed his hand over his mouth. "Yeah, your mom knows how to minimize collateral damage."

"She's a tough act to follow. I'm glad my younger sisters beat me to motherhood."

"I'm sure Billie and Goldie are wonderful mothers, but you," Chase said, a glimmer in his eyes, "you were always the nurturing one. You took care of everybody."

A smile tugged at my lips. I had happy memories of babysitting Goldie, Sage, and Billie—taking them swimming, horseback riding, and to the movies. *Not the scary ones though.*

I shook my head, a little dizzy from Chase's observation. Memories of him with my family were many and varied, only I didn't think he'd paid me much attention. "I didn't think you noticed."

He was silent for a moment, then nodded. "I did."

Afterward, our conversation slowed. He focused on his food, the muscles in his jaw flexing as he chewed. While I'd heard a little about Chase's childhood, it was nothing firsthand…nothing straight from him. I only knew his father was never around and after his mother died, his grandfather raised him and his sister.

He tipped his chin toward me. "You know, you remind me of my sister. She looked out for me, steered me away from trouble. She fixed supper when Grandpa was on second shift and taught me how to do laundry." His brows pulled together. "I think you liked helping with the younger kids, but for Carrie it was pretty much a necessity. Grandpa wasn't very motherly."

Carrie Bova—or Strickland now—was the blonde suntanned teenager every middle school girl hoped to become one day. I remembered pouring over Ace's high school yearbook, amazed her name appeared in the index almost as many times as the quarterback and student body president. Now I followed her on social media and her likes dwarfed mine. *Which is easy to do.*

"I always thought Carrie was so beautiful."

"She is." He cocked his head. "But so are you."

I crossed my feet at the ankles, toes curling again. I reached for my milkshake, grinning around the straw.

"Before you disappeared on me at the wedding," Chase said in a voice mixed with amusement and fondness, "I watched you walk away and sit down beside your mom. It's like God just clicked copy-paste on your mom when he created you. You're her in thirty years. I like your mom." He polished off his milkshake with a slurp. "I like you, too."

I uncrossed my feet and planted them flat on the floor. I needed an anchor for the riptide coursing through my body but had nothing more than my wits to go on. "You may be a world traveler, Chase Bova, but you sure haven't lost your Southern charm."

"Why, thank you, darlin'." He leaned back, folding

his arms over his chest.

"I can't imagine what it must be like to go to all those places, seeing so much of the world. What surprised you most in your travels?"

"That's easy. People." He scratched his jaw. "For as much as we differ in our cultures, we're all pretty much the same. The good and the bad of humanity."

"Not long after college, I thought about joining one of those traveling nurse programs."

"No way." He crossed his arms on the tabletop. "What stopped you?"

"I don't know. The timing just never seemed right."

"Timing?"

I nodded, awareness prickling my neck.

"Just timing?" He cocked his head. "A little vague, don't you think?"

"It means I had more important things going on in my life."

He quirked a brow. "Like what?"

"Doesn't matter." I wiggled in my chair and swiped a loose strand of hair off my cheek. "I could ask you the same question, you know. Only about home."

He half-shrugged. "You could. Fire away."

I raised my chin. "Okay, so what stopped you from coming home more often?"

"I don't know. Somehow the *timing* just never seemed right."

I folded my arms, head tilted.

"Sorry. I couldn't resist." As his mouth twitched into his devilish crooked smile, he raised his hand. "But seriously. First, I needed to make something of myself, for myself. Second, I knew growing a business and building my brand was how I was going to make that happen. Third, I was busy collecting memories, and the ones I was making on the water were a lot more fun than any I might've made here."

Chase paused for a breath, and I had to admit his honesty and candor impressed me. Outside of my dad and brothers, honest men were like a glass of lemonade in a heatwave. I looked at his hand, two fingers, two reasons left. Silence stretched between us, his expression shifting from unguarded to hopeful…maybe even a little cautious.

He raised another finger. "Carrie got married and moved away when I was eighteen." And then he ticked off the last one. "And after Grandpa died a few years ago, I just couldn't find much of a reason to return. I hired a management company to take care of the house because I wanted to keep it. But I don't know." He lowered his hand to the table, quietly drumming his fingers. "It didn't feel much like home after that."

"How about now…?"

Chase raised an eyebrow to what remained of our french fry mountain, and when I shook my head, he pushed the plate aside. Making a fist with his hands, he said, "Now's good. The *timing's* definitely right." He winked at me with ease and familiarity, and my breath hitched. "And besides, I love a big project, and that's exactly what I've got with the old place. Not so much repairs, but remodeling and updates, for sure."

I gazed at Chase, and the diner fell quiet. Shapeless tables filled with faceless people faded to gray. There was no room for dinging pinball machines and children's chatter in my mind fog.

I chewed on the corner of my lip. Chase had actually *done* the things he set out to do, and now had his razor-sharp focus on his homeplace. My world of lists and plans seemed like childish scribbling.

"I wish I knew my reasons as well as you know yours," I said, trying to drag my thoughts out of the shadows.

His smile creased the corners of his brown eyes. "I bet you know. You just don't like to talk about them, and that's okay."

I nodded, startled by his encouragement.

"Besides, you have your whole life ahead of you. You can do whatever you want."

I folded my hands in my lap, unsure of how to move forward. "You make everything sound so easy."

He chuckled. "Not really. I was just taught it doesn't matter how much time is between today and someday. What matters is that you get there."

His wisdom lifted the corners of my mouth, and I was still mulling it over as we left the Sundae Hut and climbed inside his truck. Maybe the part of me so fixated on Chase's physical attributes had overlooked his obvious intellect. The man was thoughtful, persistent, yet considerate.

One serious trifecta.

Chase watched as I snapped the seat belt in place, looking at me like I was worth the wait. On the drive back to the hospital, we talked about summer movies we both wanted to see which led to him asking me about my younger brother, Sage.

"Yeah, he's doing great. They've started filming season two of the show, and the pace is pretty intense. He's part of a great writing team, but it still takes time to put together all the episodes."

"I get it. Screenwriters are always in demand,

revising the shit that doesn't work. He's probably on his laptop around the clock."

I nodded. "Pretty much, but he's enjoying being on location again in Wilmington. He's rented a place a few blocks from the ocean and swims every morning."

He quirked an eyebrow. "You still swimming?"

"Laps in the pool every other day."

He parked his truck in a space near my car and turned toward me. "I was swimming at the fitness center earlier before I ran into you. But I'm not gonna lie, I could use a little motivation. Maybe get a few pointers. Mind if I join you in the pool sometime?"

My stomach cut a somersault. Images of Chase in swim trunks, all wet and bare chested, made my skin tingle. In my brain, I ticked through my trio of racer-back swimsuits and cringed in my seat. *Like this dress, there's nothing sexy about them.* I inhaled, then exhaled slowly. *This is not a date. He just wants an exercise buddy.*

"Sure, Chase."

A crease crowded his brow. "Uh-uh. None of that." He took my hand, squeezing it gently. "That's exactly what you said to me at the wedding reception. 'Sure, Chase,' and I believed you." I wiggled my fingers, but he held my hand firmly. "If you don't want to spend time with me, Prim, just say so. I'm a big boy."

Words were my friends. I journaled and wrote poems every day. I set many of them to music. *Why are my words deserting me with Chase…?*

"I was just thinking maybe some of your swimming mojo might rub off on me. Maybe doing laps in the pool with a strong swimmer," he said, meeting my gaze with the most dazzling smile, "might make me like it more."

Confusion coursed through me. It wasn't like I was

a complete loser, but something about sitting beside my teenage dream made me feel like a featherweight.

I took a breath and summoned my courage. "Your muscle mass is dragging you down."

"Yeah, I feel like if I don't paddle my ass off, I'm going to sink."

I bit back a smile. *Damn those rock-hard abs and muscles.*

"I'm not joking," he said, leaning forward. "If I don't move, I'm gonna drown."

"Muscles make floating harder, but maybe it's your stroke."

As if I needed a reminder Chase still held my hand, he squeezed it again, but this time with more...encouragement. He gazed at me like I was some kind of lifeline. "Maybe some strong, sexy swimmer I know could teach me something besides freestyle."

Flip a pancake. With my free hand, I rubbed my fingers over my braid. The smell of him—infused in the air inside the cab, lifting from his jacket draped over the armrest—nailed me. I breathed in his clean soap scent and lifted up a quiet little prayer. *Please, Lord, don't let this idea turn into a giant belly flop.*

My lips curved into a smile. "Let me rephrase it, then. *I'd be happy to, Chase.* My shift's over at seven tomorrow night. How about I meet you at the pool at a quarter after?"

"Now that's more like it." He grinned, then hopped out of the truck and came around to my door. With the sodium parking lot lights zinging above us, he took my hand and walked me to my car like he'd done it a hundred times. And he probably had, only with other women.

Looking ahead, I spotted an ambulance, the driver slowing and rolling down his window. *"It's Brandon,"* I mouthed to Chase, releasing his hand and hiking my bag up my shoulder.

"Hey, Prim. You doing all right tonight?" Brandon asked, glaring at Chase. "Didn't your shift end a couple hours ago?"

"It did. But I had a flat tire. And Chase helped me out."

Chase stepped forward, extending his hand. "Chase Bova. Glad to meet you. And you are—?"

"Brandon. Price. Night shift EMT." He shook Chase's hand, then pushed his glasses up higher on his nose. "You must be new to Vista Falls."

He chuckled. "Nope. Born and raised here. Left for a while. Now I'm home."

His use of the word "home" warmed my heart. Maybe like me, Chase needed his family again.

"We've known each other forever," I said for additional assurance.

Brandon nodded. "I'd be happy to follow you home, Prim."

"Oh, you don't have—"

"Good of you to offer, but don't worry. I'll see Prim home safely."

Brandon looked between me and Chase, drumming his thumbs on the steering wheel for a few seconds, before inclining his head. "You good with that, Prim?"

"Absolutely. And thanks for stopping to check on me. I appreciate it." I wondered if Brandon realized he fisted his hand. As if reading my mind, he relaxed his fingers, closed his window, and proceeded to the emergency department rear entrance.

Chase looked from me to the ambulance and back to me again. "He's interested in you."

"Brandon?" I practically choked on the name. He stepped closer, and I straightened and met his darkening gaze. "He was just looking out for a co-worker—hospital code. Besides, he's way too young for me."

While I grabbed my key ring, Chase leaned against my car. "I take it you're not into the whole cougar thing?"

Without looking his way, I unlocked my car with a press on the remote. "Ah, that would be a no."

"Good to know."

I turned toward him, tugging on the yellow "Danger—Keep Out" tape surrounding this flirty exchange. "But what if I was…?"

Chase cocked his head. "I think I could make a strong case you'd be better off with an older man."

I wasn't sure what I expected from my question, but it wasn't this. His answer zinged the air between us, urging me a step further.

"Okay, so what if Brandon was thirty-five and single?"

"Too old."

"Are you saying I need a man my own age?"

He chuckled, rubbing his chin with his fingers. "What am I going to do with you, Prim?"

I smiled. *I can think of a dozen things right about now.*

He gently took my hand between his. "I think you need a particular man. One who's about three years older than you and happens to have a birthday right after yours."

"Interesting. Well, when you find him, be sure to

send him my way."

Chase laughed, and I grinned, rather pleased my inner flirt wasn't a complete ghost.

"Get in the car, Prim. And wait for me before you pull out." I started to protest, but he held out both hands, palms up. "Hey, I'm just doing as promised and following you home." He pulled out his phone, tapped it, then handed it to me. "Address and phone number please."

I took my seat, worrying my lower lip while I typed with my thumbs. The last time I'd done this was with Avery, late one Saturday morning in the emergency department. Once the doctor had cleared him of any concussion concerns after getting nailed by an errant golf ball, Avery passed me his phone. He insisted I meet him for drinks that night. In my defense, captivated by the sexy stubble on his cheeks and steely gray gaze, I did what any woman would've done.

"Prim?"

I lifted my gaze to Chase, praying lightning wouldn't strike me twice. "Here." I passed him his phone and smiled softly. "Just so you know, I'm only doing this because I don't want to make a liar out of you."

His mouth lifted at the corners. "It's just like you to care about my reputation."

I wondered if he knew the effect his smile had on women. *Probably does.* So, what'd that make me? *Another casualty.*

"Any other reason?" He leaned toward me, hand gripping the top of my door.

"Obviously, because we're meeting at the pool, we might need to text about our schedules or something." His expression turned thoughtful, and my next question rolled off my tongue. "What's your reason for wanting it?"

Chase scratched his jaw and looked up, as if piecing together his answer in the sodium lights humming above us. His gaze slowly came back to me. "I'm going to be honest. Thorne talked to me after you left the wedding reception. He told me about the verbal ass-kicking he gave you—about working too hard and wanting you to have somebody to hang out with. Worrying about you is like his number one job."

Somebody. I lowered my head and wrapped my fingers around the steering wheel, imagining it was my brother's throat.

He lifted my chin, turning my face into the light. "Thorne gave me your number and said I should call you. He thinks you should get out more. Maybe we could go running together or catch a movie…go to karaoke one night."

It made sense now. Chase had my number. He'd had it since Saturday, only he hadn't used it. He appeared in the parking lot tonight just like the day I tumbled out of the treehouse. *In the right place at the right time.*

But I thought he was finally seeing me as me…and not Thorne's little sister. "So why'd you ask for my number when you already had it?"

"Because I wanted *you* to give it to me." As his gaze swept across my face, I was certain he could see right through me—to the awkward teenager with a body shaped like a cucumber. I shifted in my seat and reached for my braid, rubbing the blunt ends with my thumb.

"Thorne didn't plant some idea in my head about spending time with you. You did that all on your own." Chase paused long enough to push out a breath. "He knows you're safe with me, that I care about you. He just doesn't know the other stuff."

I looked at him. "Other stuff…?"

"Yeah. I like you, Prim." His fingertips brushed my skin as he slid the strap of my sundress from my arm to my shoulder. My gaze fell to where his hand lingered, the intimate gesture spreading warmth through me. "And I think maybe you like me, too."

Chapter Four

Tuesday, August 9th 7:12 p.m.
Prim

I was halfway to the pool before I spotted Chase standing by a table, dragging his T-shirt over his head. I hadn't seen him shirtless since the summer before his senior year in high school, when he and Thorne spent the month of July tinkering with Thorne's old convertible. I sucked my lip between my teeth, realizing that like a vintage wine, he'd only improved with age.

The breadth of his shoulders went on for a mile, and my gaze feasted on the lines of sinew cutting his back. Sensing his hair was messy from the drag of the shirt, he ran his hands through the unruly locks all the way to the ends. *Ends that curled into a sexy flow around his neck.* Looking at him was both a dream and a workout for my libido. As he turned to the side, my gaze stopped on his shadowed jawline then fell lower to his bicep. I came up short, hissing a breath I hoped he didn't hear.

It wasn't like I'd never seen a tattoo. Some of my friends had them. My cousin had a dragon etched over his shoulder. I'd seen dozens of them—in all shapes, colors, and sizes—on patients in the emergency department. *But seeing ink on Chase?* I fought the urge to fan my face.

As I closed the remaining distance between us, the design came into view. The bold lines and intricate swirls drew my attention, so much so I curled my hands around the strap of my duffle bag to keep from reaching out and running my fingers over it.

He turned my way and smiled. We exchanged greetings, and his gaze flickered to where mine was glued to his right bicep before it lifted. "Go ahead. I don't mind questions."

I formed my words around the knot in my throat. "Is that a shield?"

"It is."

The design of the warrior's armor was inked to perfection. For a moment, I considered it made sense—a symbol that embodied the physicality and combative elements of a man, an adventurer. But doubt tugged at my thoughts, and I sensed he was on guard for more than wild animals and reptiles.

"How long have you had it?"

He cocked his head. "About a year after things really started taking off with my business, I flew to Vegas one November to meet an old acquaintance. The deal went south pretty quick, and I felt like I needed a little assurance. The artist did an amazing job, don't you think?"

I rubbed my fingers over my collarbone. "Must've been a tough negotiation."

His gaze shifted to the lifeguard strolling past us with the cleaning net in his hand then back to me. "Yeah, it was…but not for the reasons you're thinking."

Maybe it was my intuitive nature—or my penchant for nurturing others—but I knew a story lurked behind his words. But now wasn't the time for true confessions.

"Well, I think it's very…daunting."

"From you, I was hoping for something like sexy or manly." His lips moved into a half smile. "But I can work with *daunting*."

Chase stared at me—my lips, my cheeks, then lingering on my eyes. He didn't flinch as the automated jets at one end of the recreational wading pool shot intermittent arcs of water through the air. Right about now, the heat of his gaze made me wish I had a shield of my own.

"So," I said with surprising calm. "Swimming."

Chase coughed lightly, as if remembering where we were. "Right."

"Have you stretched already?" He nodded, and I smiled. "Good. Me, too."

I stepped forward and dropped my bag on the table beside his. While Chase wasn't going to see any tattoos on my skin, I hoped my nicest aqua blue swimsuit would highlight what I considered my best physical asset…my ass. I liked to think it made up for what I lacked in the chest area, and I worked hard to keep my glutes toned.

I took a deep breath, slipping out of my running shorts and pulling my tank top over my head. As his gaze swept over me, a tingle shimmied up my spine. I looked at the fine lines flanking his eyes, loving how they softened with the smile tugging at his mouth. I steadied my breath then twisted my hair into a knot, rolled on my swim cap, and fixed my goggles over my forehead.

Several long seconds later, Chase muttered an offhanded, "Shit." He scratched his jaw, gazing down his front. "Guess I'm not wearing the right gear, huh?"

"Yeah, I'm not even gonna go there." I snickered softly, waving vaguely at the region south of his waistband. My pulse raced as I imagined how the size and weight of his junk would look snug inside some proper compression swim briefs. "But if you're already dragging through the water, you might want to lose the surfer trunks and look into something more aerodynamic."

He crossed his arms over his chest. "There's no way the Boys are gonna fit in one of those little—"

"No. No, nothing like that." The words practically tumbled out of my mouth. *You come in here with your Boys wedged inside one of those, Chase Bova, and every female will faint on the pool deck.* I worked to suppress the sexy image forming in my mind. "They're called swim *briefs*, and they're perfect for training."

"Noted." His mouth curved into a half serious, half playful grin.

"But hey, I did bring you these." I dug around in my duffle before passing him a plastic bag.

His eyes lit up with gentle amusement when he pulled out the latex cap and goggles. "You keep spares for all the guys you meet at the pool?"

His tone clearly crossed into flirtation, and judging by the glint in his eye, he expected a flirty reply. But what he couldn't know was how much I was out of my element here, like a cat stuck in a tree. *Or a maybe a girl stumbling off a treehouse ladder.*

"Hardly." The admission was true, and as his brow creased, I offered, "Just a quick trip to the sports shop at the mall." *On my lunch break, I might add.* "To be fair, there wasn't a lot to choose from in Men's XL."

"Are you kidding? I love it," he said, dangling the American flag cap on his index finger. He flicked his head to the silver mirrored goggles in his other hand.

"And these are next level."

"Can't skimp on eye protection. Ever."

He took a step toward me, warm familiarity squeezing into the chlorine-heavy space between us. "This is the nicest thing anyone's done for me in a long time. You're a really good person, Prim." His chest expanded in a deep breath, then he lowered his voice. "Which is exactly why I can't believe you don't have a man—and not *Brandon* from last night—waiting in the wings."

Maybe I did have a tattoo after all—one plastered on my forehead proclaiming *Prim's Past Her Prime*. I reined in the thought, replacing it with a more probable explanation. *Thorne and his big mouth.*

I threw him a measured look. "Hey, we better get started. You know. Laps?"

With a nod, he fell in line, putting on his gear and taking the lane to my left. I glanced over at his "sexy, manly" tattoo and let my appreciative gaze skim over his torso.

"And you do this how many times a week?" He shook out his arms like the swimmers on television, effectively halting my examination.

I waved three fingers in his direction.

"I can so do that." He rolled his shoulders, stretching the cords in his muscles. "But watch me, okay? You'll see. My body's like a damn tank in the water."

"Okay, okay." I smiled, waving my hand toward the water with exaggerated agreement. "I'm watching, Mr. Big Fisherman."

He winked, then looked forward at the lane and dove into the water.

****

So maybe Chase wasn't much of a swimmer…*yet.*

We climbed out of the pool some forty minutes later, just as the lifeguard was dimming the lights, and made our way to the dressing rooms. I emerged about fifteen minutes later—in a much cuter dress than I wore last night—and met Chase in the lobby. He handed me a bottle of water, and we both took lengthy sips.

Chase wiped his mouth with the back of his hand. "So what's the verdict? Give it to me straight."

Nothing short of putting on a few pounds was going to help his buoyancy. Plenty of muscled guys enjoyed the benefits of swimming. And so could Chase.

"You've got to face facts. You're made of muscle, not fat. I bet your BMI is under twenty-two. I think you should focus on the mental side to try to minimize the sensation of sinking. With practice, you'll grow more accustomed to how your body moves in the water."

"So, I'm not always going to lumber along like a turtle?"

I giggled, then masked it quickly. "You're not likely to break any speed records, but you can swim, Chase. Your freestyle is solid. I think you'd like the breaststroke—keeps your head up and forward. You've definitely got the legs for it."

His mouth crooked upward. "Will you teach me?"

I felt out of my element with Chase. This man had led fishing expeditions all across the country, wowing the sports world with his skill and swagger. Sweet Jesus, his *muscles* had muscles. He was a six foot two wall of hot, sexy male…and he thought I could help him swim?

Somewhere between my thoughts about his washboard abs and daunting shield tattoo, I squeaked out a shaky, "Of course."

As we walked to our cars, we made plans to meet again on Thursday evening. He pulled up short at my door, touching my elbow and turning me toward him. "What about Saturday night?"

"Working. But I could meet you at the pool after."

Chase scratched his jaw. "I wasn't asking for a swim date. I was asking for a *date* date."

My palm landed on my collarbone. "A date. With me…?"

He looked left and right, then glanced over my shoulder. "There's no one here but you." Our gazes met. "I want to spend an evening with you. I have something special in mind."

Special. I took a deep breath and sighed. It was a convenient word meant to cloud my good sense. The problem with guys like Chase was they were used to getting what they wanted. They held nothing back, using the fact they looked like sex on legs to their advantage. I bet he was used to panties dropping with that line.

He closed the space between us. "Look at me." My head snapped up. "I know what you're thinking. Don't you think I'm nervous, too?"

"No."

"No…?"

I shook my head, not wanting to say the word again.

"I'm not an asshole. I know how to treat a woman."

I averted my gaze. That fact was clearly indisputable. I'd heard plenty of stories in high school about just what all Chase Bova *knew*. And the man towering over me packed a lot more testosterone than the teenaged one ever dreamed. "That's never been a question in my mind."

"I'm no saint, but I'm not trying to play you, Prim.

That's not who I am."

I gazed into his eyes. They were dark, penetrating, stormy. "I'm sorry. It just sounds like a line, and from a player like you—"

"Look, I don't know who hurt you. If I did, I'd sure as hell crush him." His hands touched mine. "I like you, and for some crazy reason, I can't get you out of my head." He stepped away, raking his hands through his hair and cupping them around his neck. "You know, maybe you're right. This is a bad idea. You're Thorne's baby sister. I've always known I should stay away from you. I just can't figure out why I don't want to anymore."

More than anything, I wanted to believe Chase. To think his attraction to me was real. My heart pinched inside my chest, daring me to cast off my insecurities. I swallowed past a lump in my throat. "I haven't been his baby sister in a long time."

He drew down his eyebrows. "Believe me, I know."

I thought about the many nights I'd spent alone since my breakup with Avery. There was no way I was going to change out the shelf liners in my kitchen cabinets again. I had no more peace lilies to transplant, and I'd already cleaned the scuffs off every pair of shoes in my closet…even my gardening clogs. My empty social calendar chugged through my brain. What's next? *Playing solitaire…?*

I straightened, wanting to speak before I chickened out and crawled back into my shell. "So, I'm off on Friday. I don't have any plans."

A smile pulled at his mouth, and his expression turned softer under the blue lights in the parking lot. "You do now. With me." He took my hand and gently squeezed it. "I promise to be a gentleman and show you a good time."

I believed the part about a good time. *'Cause hello...Chase is charming and hot as hell.* But as for being a gentleman, I pushed the thought aside. He'd starred in my fantasies since I was old enough to know how to touch myself. At thirty-one, I didn't necessarily want or need him to be a gentleman. Maybe we could hook up for the summer or slide into a friends-with-benefits arrangement. I'd been looking for love as long as I could remember. Maybe I needed to ditch the dreams and give reality a chance.

With these thoughts still rattling my brain, Chase took my bag off my arm, placed it on the passenger seat, and helped me into my car. "I'll pick you up at seven."

"Want to tell me where we're going so I'll know what to wear?"

He made a circuit over my face. "It's a surprise. We'll be outdoors—for part of the evening anyway. Just pick something you like, something comfortable."

"Pajamas...?" He quirked an eyebrow, and I giggled behind my hand. I'd forgotten what it felt like to be desired, much less pursued. A fizzy excitement whirled inside my belly, and I took a steadying breath, figuring I needed to outrun my thoughts or risk being trampled by them.

I gave him a playful salute. "Comfortable. Got it."

I started the engine, and Chase took a step back, rubbing his chin. His gaze roamed over my car. "You know they discontinued this model like a decade ago."

"Which makes her *vintage*."

"Which is a polite way of saying she's old. How many miles?"

"Chase," I tsked, tilting my head. "That's like asking

a woman how much she weighs. Ellie's more than her mileage."

He tilted his face to the sky and laughed. "Are you serious? Ellie...? You named your Elemental, *Ellie*?"

My chin dropped. "What...? It's a perfect name! Like you haven't named all your cars and boats?" He tilted his head left, then right, an obvious yes no. "And your penis?"

His eyebrows shot straight to his hairline.

Flip a pancake! What did I just say...? I shrugged it off, hiding a smile. "Oh, don't act so surprised. Guys in college talked about it all the time."

Chase planted his hands on my door, and suddenly the air felt sensual and heavy. "Guess that's a difference between me and a *college boy*." He chided, casting me a sin-dark smile. "If I'd given my penis a name, I sure as hell wouldn't go around talking about it."

I could practically feel the pink rising in my cheeks but didn't dare look away.

"But I can tell you this much. If I ever wanted my dick to have a name, you'd be the only woman I'd let do it."

I squeezed my thighs together against the tingling there. "Oh, so it's like a privilege?"

"A privilege, a promise, and for damn sure, it'd be my pleasure."

I tucked my hair behind my ear, wedging my bottom lip between my teeth. "I'm not sure we should be talking like this."

"Maybe." His grin was a little dirty and utterly beautiful. "But I think you kinda like it."

Somehow my heart and stomach smiled in unison, and I looked up at his lightly mussed hair.

"Come here." He followed my command, and I smoothed my hand over a piece of hair sticking out over his ear. I didn't care if I was being forward. I wanted to touch him. *And I think you kinda like it.*

The right corner of his mouth lifted. "So we're on for Friday night?"

"Yes."

"Good." His voice hummed with satisfaction, and he waved his finger at me. "And don't you and Ellie get any ideas about racing off from here. I'll be following right behind you. All the way home."

I smiled. Chase was gorgeous and sweet, and deep down, a protector at heart.

I'm counting on that, Chase. I'm counting on you...

Chapter Five

Friday, August 12th 11:30 a.m.
Chase

There was a time when I loved sitting down to shoot
the shit with a reporter, especially when I got to do it over
a couple of beers in some sports bar. But like most
rookies in their first interviews, I made my share of
mistakes. Whenever I thought about the early days of
starting Chase n' Dreams, I had to remind myself twenty-
year-old me was basically equal parts testosterone and
bullshit.

As I adjusted my microphone in preparation for
today's interview—a no-frills online guest spot on
Carolina Outdoors Daily—I shook my head, recalling
the time I did a segment on sports radio the week after
Halloween.

As a kid, I remembered girls trick-or-treating as
black cats and fairy princesses. But for a guy living out
of a camper with his buddies, rolling into a different river
town and its best tavern every other week, I gained a new
appreciation for Halloween parties.

Sexy cheetahs, wild jungle princesses—and one
very hot Aphrodite—came to mind. At the end of the
night, the goddess of love took first place in a costume
contest when she lifted her toga and flashed the rosebud

tattoo on her right butt cheek to the judges. Though I didn't understand why the holiday inspired otherwise reserved women to showcase their goods like bottles of expensive booze, I certainly appreciated it. And when I'd said as much on air, I got blasted by a lot of listeners. And my sponsor was pissed.

Not my best moment.

After a couple less than stellar interviews, I got better at controlling my loose lips. I learned the importance of image and branding, which in turn, meant I seldom said what was really on my mind. Journalists asked questions, and I gave them answers. The ones listeners wanted to hear. Ones that teased and left them wanting more.

Honestly, I think most people are either crazy or stupid.

"And we've got ourselves a real treat, folks. We're talking today with Chase n' Dreams founder, Chase Bova."

I slapped on a smile. *Need I say more?*

The guy coming at me through my laptop screen was a piece of work, some communications guru my sponsor hired this past spring. His name was Dick Puffer.

Yeah. No shit.

He'd introduced himself before we went on air, and for a moment, I worried I might turn blue from the laughter bottled up in my chest. Maybe if his parents had given him a solid first name, he could've managed some kind of cool wordplay, like John 'The Weed' Puffer. But *Dick...?*

Turns out the guy was some marketing whiz at Poseidon Kayaks, called in at the eleventh hour when Mitch, the regular show host, checked out with a nasty stomach flu. I knew Mitch. Mitch was a lot like me—an uncomplicated guy, at home in flannel and muddy boots, who loved jetting through the water and floating on it in equal measure. He wore his blond hair slicked back in a ponytail, but while his skin was a landscape of ink, mine was suntanned with only the one tattoo. *Yeah, I could relate to Mitch.*

I turned away, coughing the shock from my throat. I reached for my water bottle, tipped it to my lips, then settled into my chair. I took stock of the perspiration dotting Dick's forehead, the limp comb-over hair, and pale skin. No way this guy's feet had ever touched the pedals inside a kayak. Probably spent most of his time behind a laptop studying SEO analytics. But then with that name, he probably found making friends with computer code a lot easier than people.

I screwed the cap on the water and looked into the camera. I reminded myself none of this was my problem. This live cast was part of my contract, which meant ole Dick had dibs on me for the next half hour.

"So tell me. Most guys dream of retiring and going fishing all day long in a Poseidon kayak. What's it been like spending a career in one?"

I chuckled at the twist on an expected question. While my transition from being the face of Chase n' Dreams was still a work in progress, I knew how to talk-up the sponsor.

"It's been an amazing ride, and while I'm moving into the production side of the house, I'll still be very involved with my business. Lots of trips to plan and navigate for the crew. But I can promise you one thing. I'll always find time to be on the water in my Poseidon 21X."

Dick chimed his agreement before rehashing some of the details of my last tour down the Santee River. He framed a few more questions around navigating weather patterns and critiquing various types of bait, and I gave him textbook responses. For a guy with a tragic name, he did a decent job with the questions.

When Dick scratched his jaw and cleared his throat, I gripped the seat of my chair with both hands. I sensed the change in his tone before the words left his mouth.

"Your support of charitable causes is no secret, Chase. But your contributions for cancer research, well, that's personal, isn't it?"

Once again, I'd nailed it. And though I'd answered the question a dozen times before, it never failed to pinch my heart. "It is."

"I understand you were only a boy when your mother passed."

I nodded. "Brain cancer. Super aggressive. She died within a year of her diagnosis."

"That must have been hard."

A creek stone is hard. This is fucking granite. I was a kid, and God diced my heart into confetti. *Is that the best you've got, Dick?*

While I swallowed more water, I formed my response. "It was. But thankfully, my family came together afterward—we really supported one another." *Grandpa, Carrie, and me...not my loser father.* "I just want to honor my mom's memory and hopefully help others who are battling cancer—or fighting it alongside a loved one."

"It's a great thing you're doing, Chase. You're an inspiration to all of your fans. And to all of us here at Poseidon, too."

I nodded, rubbing my hand over my neck, and took a deep breath. It wasn't easy accepting praise for doing what was right. The way I looked at it, maybe I could save some other kid out there from losing his mom to cancer. Supporting research was the right thing to do, and I had money enough to do it. End of story. But again, I hardly ever said what was on my mind.

So I thanked Dick for his acknowledgement, then turned the conversation toward the good work Poseidon Kayaks did for other charitable causes. The last few minutes of the interview passed with no bumps or hitches. After he signaled the live cast feed had ended, we exchanged a few words, then I tipped my head and closed my laptop.

I rubbed my palms over my eyes and groaned under my breath. I leaned back in my chair, and thumbing through my phone, spotted a message from Thorne. I opened it, then grabbed my keys and headed out the door.

****

Ever since Thorne had talked to me at the wedding about spending time with Prim, I'd been nursing a slow burn in the pit of my stomach. He had no idea his little sister had always been on my radar or that I'd avoided her in high school. Sure, I often swung by the pool on the chance I'd see her swimming in the lanes, and even occasionally hung out longer than needed when we worked on the convertible. But I'd quit sleeping over once we got to middle school, because the chance she might see me with my morning boner hit too close to home.

Truth was I'd always liked Prim—in a buggy-kid-sister way—until that summer before she started her freshman year, and she grew curves that sloped into a particularly perfect tight ass. I didn't know if it was the hundred or so laps in the pool or the thousand kicks of her legs that gave those cheeks their perfect shape and it didn't matter. Because thinking of Prim as anything other than Thorne's baby sister was unthinkable, pointless, and utterly despicable. I thought with my dick in those days, and it had no business being anywhere near Primrose Vreeland.

I pulled my truck into an open spot at the library and made my way inside. Like the maybe dozen times I'd come here as a kid, I noticed the air still smelled of paper, lemon wood polish, and vinyl.

I walked past rows of metal bookcases and several artificial Ficus plants and gave a nod to the librarian standing behind a computer. As his mouth twisted, I glanced down at my faded jeans and the cuffs of my Henley shirt shoved up my forearms. By the heat of his gaze, he clearly thought I was lost—or even worse, some vagrant looking for a public restroom.

I chuckled under my breath and continued down the glass-walled hallway, glancing into each of the study rooms. *Nope. Nope.* I cut the corner and picked up my pace. *Where the hell are you?*

In the next moment, I heard the lilting giggle of a female voice followed by a deep muffled tone. I walked toward the sounds, stopping at a room where a brunette stood—no, make that leaned—suggestively against a table, a thick book clutched against her chest.

Thorne spotted me, and I was instantly transported to our high school days. Back then, my best friend spent a good amount of time with his head stuck in the middle of a book, blissfully unaware of just how many girls wished they could swap places with said book. I realized he was just as oblivious today as he was then. The woman's gaze followed Thorne's, and she straightened when she saw me.

I stepped into the doorway, scratching my jaw and shaking my head at the array of books and notepads littering the table. With a pencil wedged behind his ear, the only thing missing was a tweed cardigan.

"I thought researchers just looked up stuff online these days," I said, deadpan.

"Hell, no." Thorne pushed away from the desk, rolling his chair backward, then smiled. "Well, not the good ones anyway."

I laughed, and the woman standing between us shifted her weight from one side to the other, before passing the book to Thorne. "Well, here's the volume you were looking for, Mr. Vreeland."

"Thorne." He corrected, missing the blush rising in her cheeks as he thumbed through the book. "Thanks, again."

"Any time…Thorne." The stress she gave to his name mimicked bright red puffy hearts in a cartoon. She slipped quietly from the room, but I caught her looking back over her shoulder at him.

"You could've had your way with her, you know that, right?" I gazed at the glass walls around the room— with no blinds—then added, "Well…not *here* maybe, but—"

Thorne laughed then removed his smart-guy glasses. I was glad to see he'd traded up from his high school jock wire-rims to sleek gunmetal gray frames. Women liked men in glasses, especially when they had the brains to match them, although I doubted my friend had given either of these things much thought.

I rolled over a chair, flipped it around, and sat, folding my arms over its back. "Did you at least get her name?"

Thorne tugged his ear, and the pencil dropped on his lap. Without looking at me, he put it on the table. "She's just doing her job."

"So you don't have a name."

"Lacie. No. It's Kacie…I think." I raised my brows, and he mumbled, "Fuck you." By way of explanation, he gestured to the book in his hand. "She—"

"You mean, Kacie-I-think?" I laughed as he flipped me his middle finger.

"—did spend a lot of time looking for this."

"Pretty sure she'd sell her kidney if she thought it'd get her closer to you. You'd know this if you took a look around once in a while."

Thorne grunted and rolled his chair back to the table. "So, you texted me earlier." He reached for his glasses and slid them into place. "What's up?"

I remembered the text and briefly questioned my sanity. Why was I doing this? Oh yeah, because Thorne was my best friend, and I didn't want any weird shit between us.

"I did what you asked. I talked to Prim." I shifted in my seat. *This is going to be about as much fun as plunging a toilet.*

Thorne looked up, rolling his pencil between his fingers.

"She's helping me with swimming." I read the question in his brows. "I'm still running some. But I like the workout in the pool—better on the knees, you know."

"Well. Sounds good."

"So, I ran into her the other day at the fitness center."

With a flat tire and an even flatter spirit. "Then we grabbed a bite at the Sundae Hut. Talked some." *And I made her smile…a couple times, actually.*

I watched as Thorne flipped through the book Kacie-I-Think brought him before pressing on. "Then we met at the pool again. You know, she's still a really great swimmer." Thorne hummed his agreement, and on a single breath, I formed my next sentence in my head before cutting it loose. "And afterward, I asked her out…for tonight."

Thorne lifted his gaze, his finger curled around the corner of a page. "Out?"

My arms tightened over the back of the chair. "You wanted her to have somebody to hang out with, right?"

Thorne sat up taller. "You're meeting her for karaoke night…with friends?"

"No."

His hands left the book, and he placed them, palms down, on the table. "She likes movies, but nothing—"

"Scary. Yeah, I remember."

Thorne leaned back in his chair, surprise marking his brow, and my stomach nosedived to my feet. *Shit.*

I ran my hands through my hair and cupped them around my neck, chuckling. "Jesus, don't you remember that Halloween your dad took all of us to the haunted corn maze?" He nodded once. "And how Ace gave her hell for staying home with your mom and the little kids?" He nodded again, and I shrugged. "So I paid attention."

His gaze narrowed. "I talked to Prim this morning, and she didn't mention any of this. It must not be a big deal."

"Maybe." I squeezed as much respect as I could into my tone before continuing, "But it's kind of a big deal to me. That's why I'm here."

Thorne knocked his pencil on the table a few times. "Does 'hang out' mean the same thing to you as it does to me?"

I thought about his question for a few beats. The life I'd lived on the road wasn't the kind women found comforting. But then I'd never really wanted to hang out with a woman for more than a couple days.

But Prim felt different. She *was* different. Thoughts of being alone with her had descended over me the past few days. This kind of thinking was as foreign to me as sitting down to a home-cooked meal. I'd never had everything I wanted all together in the same place at the same time, and I wasn't quite sure what to do with that feeling.

"I think so. But maybe the better question is does hanging out mean the same thing for me as it does to Prim." I stared at Thorne, the guy who'd stuck with me through thin and thinner. I needed him to understand my interest in Prim wasn't about what I wanted. She held the power, controlled the reins.

"She knows I like her and that I want to get to know her better. I've also made it clear I'm not some jerk. This is not about scoring with my best friend's sister." I purposefully left out the word "baby" because Prim was a grown damn woman. "So, she and I are good." I met his gaze, ready to take his best shot. "How about us? Are we good?"

Thorne snapped his pencil in two. "Dammit, Chase. This wasn't what I had in mind. At all." He tossed the pieces toward the trashcan by the door...and missed. "Prim's not in a good place right now. The last guy she was with screwed her over so bad she won't even talk about it. I thought you could be a friend to her, be somebody to get her social life going again. Introduce her to some people."

"Jesus, I haven't lived in Vista Falls for years. Who the hell am I hanging out with?"

"People flock to you no matter where you go, and you know it."

I closed my mouth, rubbing a palm across it. For some reason being labeled the guy I'd always been stung like a slap in the face. "Sorry I'm not much for crowds these days, shooting darts and chasing skirts."

Several seconds stretched between us before Thorne spoke. "You've known Prim her whole life, you know how she is. Gentle…yet tough as a little bulldozer. So fucking kind and forgiving to everyone…even the little shits who mess with her heart." He shook his head. "No. Not once—not *ever* have you been interested in a girl like my sister."

But I had been interested…only I'd left it alone. Because high school Chase Bova only wanted to get laid.

With a voice like one of those estate sale auctioneers, Thorne ticked off the names of girls I'd messed around with in school. I stared at him, this guy who'd witnessed most of my teenage bad behavior, shrinking under a fresh coat of self-loathing.

And it wasn't like I'd changed my ways in my twenties either.

While I was still the same guy—only now in my thirties—I wasn't *that* same guy. Only Thorne didn't know that. *Hell, I'm still trying to figure it out…but it has something to do with your sister.*

I cupped my fingers over my mouth and blew the air from my cheeks. "You're right. My track record is shit, and it makes no sense for my name to be with hers in the same sentence. But I would've talked to her on my own, Thorne. I decided that while I was listening to her sing at the reception. You're not responsible for this."

"If it goes south, I will be. And there won't be a creek bank remote enough for you to hide from me. I'd hate to have to track down my best friend, but I'll damn well do it if you hurt Prim in any way."

"Which is exactly why I stayed miles away from her in high school."

"What the fuck?"

I cleared my throat, choosing my next words carefully. "I noticed her, all right? But I wasn't stupid. She was out of my league."

"Still is. Sorry, man, but it's the truth."

I threw my head back, mentally counting the fiberglass ceiling tiles in the room, and sighed. *Hard to fucking argue with that.*

Finally, I looked across the table and met his quiet gaze. "I guess I just wanted you to know what I was doing, how I was feeling. I can't control how you feel about it. You've made protecting Prim your life's work, so it makes sense you're wary, even of me."

"Especially of you." Though he huffed the words, a tiny movement at the corner of his mouth caught my attention.

I planted my palms on the table. "I like her, man. That much I can say for sure. And you know how I am about the people I care about—I mean *truly* care about." He nodded, and I seized the moment. "Look. I swear to God I'll be nice and polite, a gentleman at—"

"You'd better keep it PG," he said, air pointing at me.

I leaned forward. "How about PG-13? I mean, we are adults." He nailed me with a don't-fucking-push-me glare, and I laughed. Then he laughed…and at least some of the awkward slipped out of the room.

"Thanks. You know…for telling me what's going on." Thorne scratched his jaw. "You didn't have to do that."

I pushed out of my chair and stood, hands by my sides. "I've never lied to you. I needed you to know the truth before I take Prim out tonight. So I can relax and enjoy getting to know her better."

He closed his eyes, huffing, waving me off. "Will you just please get the hell out of here before I change my mind?"

I backed away slowly, grinning, jerking my thumb toward the door. "Hey, you want me to go find Kacie-I-Think…?"

As Thorne wadded a piece of paper into a ball, I ducked out the door. I looked at him through the glass and, spotting the good-natured smile never too far from his face, grinned and mouthed, "*Nice shot.*"

Chapter Six

Friday, August 12th 5:40 p.m.
Prim

This much water couldn't have come from a single kitchen pipe. It was a scientific—*plop!*—and mathematical—*slosh!*—impossibility. Clearly there were a number of things rusty and outdated about this house, but water pressure wasn't one of them. With a broom in my hand, I dragged my feet through the wading pool of my kitchen floor, sweeping the mucky mess out the door.

After a yoga class that'd left happy hormones in complete control of my body, I returned home to *this*. Flipping Niagara Falls, water thundering from the cabinet below the kitchen sink like some alien escaping its chains.

Move over serotonin. Stress hormone cortisol reporting for duty.

After swabbing the deck for at least an hour, I stopped, whooshing out a breath and leaning on the broom handle. I dragged my hand over my forehead and pushed the sweat beads into my hair. I glared at every piece of fabric I'd tossed from my cabinets onto the floor, now a bunch of wet blobs connected by little meandering streams.

My gaze swung to the clock on the stove—*shit!*—and my dread meter ticked up a notch. I was anxious about this date before yoga, but now—in all my slimy glory—I was a pin cushion of nerves. I dipped my head and took a whiff of my armpits, cringing.

My ears pricked at the rumble of truck tires on gravel and the faint squeal of brakes in need of replacement. Then the engine went silent.

And every coherent thought in my brain dropped.

Like a call in a dead zone.

I started laughing, awkwardly, a muddled mix of desperation and irony spilling out of my mouth. How could it be possible the world would serve me up on a platter—looking like a modern-day scullery maid in soggy yoga pants and a sports bra—to *this* guy?

I stashed the broom in the corner, grabbed my phone, and snapped a selfie. I gazed at it, at the mascara smudges on my cheeks and hairs frizzing around my headband. *Yeah, there's got to be a really good song hiding somewhere in this shitshow.*

Resigned, I closed my phone and hopped onto the kitchen bar. I let my legs thump against the cabinets while I waited for the stomp of feet climbing—*one, two, three, four*—steps. A single hand made a solid knock on the screen door, and I took a deep breath, calling out, "Come on in."

After the sound of more footsteps, Chase pulled up beside me, stopping short of the linoleum swamp. I turned my head toward him. He was wearing cowboy boots. *I like boots.* He wore a white button-down shirt tucked into dark blue jeans, the denim worn just enough to hug his tight ass in the best possible way. *And I really like shirts and jeans, too.* And in his hands, a bouquet of sunflowers. *Thank you. These just really make me…happy.*

The sight of him standing in my rental house with its 1990s mauve and blue kitchen did funny things to my belly. He smelled of freshly washed skin and shampoo, a complete contrast to me and my stinky armpits.

Chase handed me the flowers. "Got a bigger broom?"

I watched him unbuttoning his sleeves with growing interest, rolling them up to expose sturdy forearms. "Not sure. If there is, it'd be in the storage—" My voice fell as he bee-lined it toward the carport. After a series of dings and thumps, he returned with a giant stiff-edge broom.

I mean, who knew…?

While Chase brushed the remaining water out the door, I placed the sunflowers in a ceramic vase. I turned, and leaning against the counter, watched the steady repetitive push and pull of his back and shoulder muscles. When he turned his head and caught me ogling him, his mouth twitched. And for one brief moment, our gazes met, exchanging in some kind of silent language all their own.

We grabbed armfuls of wet towels, and he followed me to the washing machine. I started the load, then closed the sliding laundry room door.

I swung around to Chase and, with his body completely blocking the overhead light, took a backward step. As my eyes adjusted to the white cotton fabric stretched across his chest, I squeaked a breath, pointing. "Um, your shirt."

His gaze dropped, then slowly lifted to mine.

As I drew my lip between my teeth, I heard him take his next breath. A heavy one. And I tried to ignore what the husky sound did to my insides. "Why am I always getting your shirts wet?"

He chuckled, his dimple marking his cheek. "You do know there are simpler ways to get me shirtless, right? And I'm not talking about swimming, either."

I giggled and folded my arms under my breasts, studying his face, deciding the word "handsome" was simply unworthy of the man.

I tilted my head to one side. "Something simpler than tears or a kitchen flood?"

He nodded, and I felt his gaze skim over my skin and damp hair before he took my hand. "So, how about we get this date night started?"

I blinked.

"I'll wait for you to get ready."

Wait?

Like here?

Chase walked me to the den, then dropped my hand. He sat down on the velveteen chair and reached for the recliner lever, frowning when it spun around on its hinges.

"It's broken."

He dropped his hands to his knees and winked. "Bet I can fix it…after I figure out what's happening with your kitchen pipes."

I was beginning to like his teasing tone—and the way the right corner of his mouth lifted when he used it—a little too much. They were beautiful.

God, *he* was beautiful.

But while Chase was incredibly nice to look at, he was even nicer to be around. And not just because he did sexy man things so well and clearly possessed the superpower of fitting square pegs into round holes. His every word, every action, warmed me like a wool blanket on an October hayride, and if I wasn't careful, I might start wanting more moments like this with him…flood waters and all.

I shifted, trying to hide the crush of embarrassment in my face. "On the plus side, the place came furnished, and most things actually do work." I squinted, nose wrinkled. "Just maybe not the sink…and the recliner…and the pantry door that won't shut…and—"

"Prim."

I blinked and our gazes locked.

"Hey, it's just me. I've got this. Now go get ready, okay?"

My chest rose and fell, then somehow, I managed a nod and disappeared into the bathroom.

****

Chase

I knew this was a furnished rental house, but it didn't matter. This was Prim's place, her let-down-your-hair and faded T-shirt space, and it smelled like her…vanilla with a hint of tangerine.

As she started the shower, I got to work. I quickly reconnected the spring rod underneath the recliner and tested it out—*yep, good as new*—then set out for the kitchen. A quick inspection under the sink confirmed a corroded pipe was at fault, something I—or either of her brothers—could fix in a snap. *But I've got this one.* And honestly, I knew I'd get her next mishap, too.

And the one after that if she'll let me.

I made my way back to the den. I let my gaze travel the room, spotting a guitar in a stand in one corner and an armchair with a cushioned ottoman in the other. A string of framed photos filled the mantel over the fireplace, and I stopped at each one, studying the various moments of Prim's life. Obviously, I remembered the braids from when she was a kid, and there she was wearing them in a photo taken at the beach perched on her dad's shoulders. I shook my head. *How God takes a dad like Gray Vreeland so soon, while leaving behind a dirtbag one like Curt Bova, makes no sense to me.*

I moved on to a teenage photo of Prim and her sister, Goldie, in matching black swimsuits, medals draped around their necks. Next, I spotted a frame with her college's name on it. Prim stood at the center of a group of friends wearing painter overalls and a ponytail, her cheek speckled with paint. I leaned forward and read the caption at the bottom of the photo—*Spring Break Spring Cleaning Fundraiser.*

As the shower stopped, I made my way through the last of her photographs. I dropped onto the sofa, bouncing my knee and slicing my hand through my hair, and wondered about pictures of ex-boyfriends. Selfishly, I hoped she'd deleted them from her phone—or at least had them tagged in an album called 'Dickheads.'

Prim turned on her hairdryer and the low buzz filled the house. Was it crazy I wanted to know what kind of guys she'd been attracted to, how I measured up? Maybe my talk with Thorne had all this shit stirred up in my head. *That has to be it.* Because I never got like this, and I never had jealous thoughts about women. I didn't know what any of this meant. I only knew my thoughts were honest fucking real.

I sensed her gaze on me, caught her scent in the air, a few moments before I looked her way.

Holy God.

While some women had to do a lot to grab a guy's

attention, it took little for Prim to stop me in my tracks. Her hair fell in soft waves down her back, and her pink lips curved into a gentle smile. She wore ass-hugging blue jeans with a loose fitting top and tan sandals. She looked so damn wholesome, like she belonged on a billboard for one of those North Carolina mountain apple orchards. But not tonight. *Tonight you belong to me.*

Chapter Seven

Friday, August 12th 7:05 p.m.
Prim

My nerves ran hot and cold at the same time, my
history with guys a rerun in my head as Chase pulled out
of my driveway. He asked me to choose where we went,
and I wanted it to be someplace new, something different
from places we'd known as kids—a dorky kid-sister-free
zone.

So, I directed him to my new favorite pizza place a
few blocks away. Housed in a renovated red brick
warehouse, the place had exposed pipes and an actual
bar-length chalkboard with about forty craft beers on tap
spelled out in neon colored chalk.

I'd made fast friends with the owner, Tony, months
ago because well...I loved pizza. But it turned out we
also had a lot in common. He was a retired studio
producer from Nashville and had worked with many
legendary country music singers. As such, he had the
walls filled with music memorabilia and signed
caricatures of artists he'd collaborated with over his
thirty-year career. He liked to tell stories about the music
business, and being a songwriter at heart, I enjoyed
listening to him.

After spotting me at the restaurant entrance, Tony
welcomed us, and I introduced him to Chase.

Tony seated us at a cozy corner booth. "I got the recording you sent me last week. I liked it."

I felt color pinking my cheeks. "Really?"

"You got any more?" When I nodded, he added, "Well, send them my way when you can. Now," he said, giving us menus, "I hope you two enjoy your evening."

A few minutes later, a server took our pizza and drink orders.

"Look at you, Primrose. A nurse by day, and singer songwriter by night."

I crossed my arms on the tabletop. "I do it for me. I don't even know why I shared anything with Tony, except he wouldn't stop pestering me about it."

"Well, if your voice is any indication of your talent, the songs you've written must kick ass. Don't forget I heard you at Brent's wedding." He paused, the corner of his mouth pulling up into a bashful grin. "You have a beautiful voice."

Suddenly, my insides went all warm and soft. I remembered how nervous I was at the reception, knowing Chase was listening to me sing. A small surge of pride filled my chest that he'd liked what he heard.

Our server returned with our beers, and Chase smiled, showing a tiny glint of teeth, and leaned toward me. "Can't wait to try this one. I gotta love a brew named 'Little River.' "

"I thought you might pick that one... or maybe 'Fresh Catch.' "

"Next round." He winked. "And I can't think of a better choice than 'Lifeline' for you."

"I like it because it's not too hoppy, but I suppose the name fits. When you work in emergency, you get a lot of that stuff. People think we're invincible, sort of miracle workers."

A crease marked his brow. "But you kinda are."

"Please don't think I take it as an insult—I mean, it's true a lot of the time. And I love what I do." I crossed my arms on the tabletop, tilting my head. "It's just…well, there's me the nurse…and me the sister and daughter…" My breath hitched. I wasn't even sure where I was going with this, but then his eyes softened, encouraging, and I met his gaze. I wanted—I mean, really wanted—him to understand. "And then there's just *me* me."

Two buckets sat on every table—one filled with peanuts and the other one for the empty shells—and Chase tipped it in my direction. I grabbed a few peanuts, and he did the same, and we began popping open shells.

Chase chewed quietly. "I get what you mean about people only seeing what they want to see. It's all they've got to go on though, unless you let them in. Show them what really makes you tick."

I nodded, and tucking my hair behind my ear, we continued talking over peanuts and beer. I couldn't help but notice how conversation came easy to Chase, his personality as natural as sunshine bouncing on lake water. I'd known him my whole life, but only now was I seeing him for myself. *And not through Thorne, social media buzz, the local rumor mill, or my geeky adolescent imagination.*

When our pizza arrived, Chase stared at the dozen toppings stretched all the way out to the crust. He gave a low-pitched whistle. "I can see why they call it *The Kitchen Sink.*"

I bit my lip, grinning. "I told you it was next level."

As we dove into the pizza, Chase asked me questions and listened. The way he gazed into my eyes made my pulse hum through my body. No man had ever taken such an interest in my vanilla life, and before long, a stunning truth nailed me square in the face.

There were men out there in the world—real, heterosexual men—who *actually* listened…?

Flip.

A.

Pancake.

With this realization still knocking around in my brain, I returned the gesture, asking Chase some questions. Though he shared a little about his adventures on the water, he smiled the most when he talked about his sister and niece. The expression was impossible to miss, tugging on his mouth while he pulled at the cheese on the pizza.

Even the way he chewed was sexy, a heady mix of warm comfortable masculinity, so very different from Avery. The Ass lived a paint-by-number life, and he set the colors to suit his mood. I'd never once seen him in a jam either—*like sweeping water from a kitchen while dressed in nice clothes.* Something made me think he'd have found a way to blame the unfortunate mishap on me.

The next hour passed in a sweet blur, and after dinner, Chase drove us toward town, parking in the lot near the post office.

He turned off the engine and turned to me. "Don't move."

I nodded, my gaze following him as he walked around the truck and opened my door. He helped me down, grabbed his backpack from the cab, and slung it over his shoulder. Without hesitation, he took my hand in his, threading our fingers together, and led us toward the town square. As I reminded myself he was a friend, I couldn't help but feel stars where our skin touched.

A smile started on one side of Chase's perfect mouth, sliding into place in a matter of seconds. "I guess you know about the old films they're showing on Friday nights."

He'd been in Vista Falls for all of ten days and knew more about what was happening than I did. But I played along. "Yeah, I think I heard about it."

He looked my way. "You like musicals?"

"Of course, but I think the better question is, do you?"

He laughed and squeezed my hand. "I like the classics—war movies, dramas, even the occasional musical."

I'd barely begun to process this when he brought us to a stop—where a gigantic screen stood in front of the courthouse—and pulled a blanket from his backpack. An older couple sat side by side in a pair of camping chairs to our right, and several families sprawled out in the space in front of us. The air held the scent of buttery popcorn from a nearby vendor and one soap-clean guy. Chase fanned the blanket over the lawn and motioned for me to sit down, then he joined me, a couple of cushions in his hands.

I raised up so he could slide one under me, then he sat down on the other, sliding in so close our elbows brushed. When the film started, and as the music filled the space between us, something else lingered there, unspoken but in no way silent.

Chase turned his hand over on my knee, and within seconds, I felt his gaze on me. Fizzy excitement bubbled through my veins. Was he always like this, touching and turning toward the woman he was with…?

I looked at his gentle expectant expression and felt instantly calmed, wanted. I took his hand, rubbing and studying every crease and callous, knowing it was capable of tackling the worst kitchen catastrophe…and experienced in traversing the curves of a woman's body. Many women's bodies.

I took a steadying breath. *Maybe even* my *body.*

"Hey," Chase said, his voice a deep whisper.

"Hey." I held his gaze for several spectacular seconds. It'd be so like me to retreat now, refuse to acknowledge the attraction thrumming between us. Because I didn't like being vulnerable…didn't want to be let down again.

His mouth twitched, softness playing around the edges of his smile. "I like your hands, too."

"You do?"

"Yeah." He lifted my hand to his lips and kissed my knuckles. Then he wove our fingers together, placing our joined hands on my thigh. "I like all of you."

My stomach flipped.

Was I crazy to open my heart to this man? *Yep.* Could I stop this even if I wanted to? *Not a chance.*

Chase Bova had me. And I wanted to live in that feeling, at least for tonight.

****

Chase

Sweet. Jesus. When my lips touched Prim's soft knuckles, they tingled. And the world felt completely fucking *right*.

I quickly lost count of the songs in the movie because my brain was occupied with more important things. Like when I would kiss her again…and where.

And how impossibly small her feet were and how her hair was just so damn thick and pretty.

Somewhere near the end of the movie, she kicked off her sandals and curled up beside me, her arm a pillow under her head. I did the same—except I kept my boots on—and laid down behind her. I kept a good foot of space between us, safe for a public place and true to my promise to Thorne.

I took the long way to her house because I just didn't want the night to be over. I even found myself telling her about my plans for Grandpa's house—pretty shocking considering I hadn't told anyone, not even my sister.

I parked in Prim's driveway and walked with her up the sidewalk, noting the pair of foot lamps that needed replacing. *I'll get them when I get the parts to repair your sink.*

Prim stopped on the third step and sat down. The moonlight shimmered on her cheeks, making her look like the earth angel she'd always been.

Even when I was in high school, I'd never done first dates right. Things like protective fathers were a red flag, and I dodged them at every turn. But I wasn't a reckless guy anymore. I liked spending time with Prim more than I thought I would, and by God, I was going to see this date through to a respectable end.

She gazed at me, gathering her hair in her hand and pulling it over one shoulder. "So earlier, when you were telling me about your grandpa's house, I was wondering how many more acres you bought."

I crossed my arms. "All ten acres behind the place."

"Wow, guess you really are planning on settling down."

"Pretty much. I love Chase n' Dreams, and it's been

an amazing ride, but the years have a way of catching up with a man. I wanted to go out on top, on my terms. As a producer and consultant, I can stay relevant without having to log all the hours in the field."

"Sounds like you're going to have your hands full between that and your remodeling."

Since boredom wasn't an option, that was the plan. Refurbish the home and honor Grandpa's memory. Spend time getting to know my beautiful niece. Give my relationship with my big sister some long overdue attention.

"I want to fix up the place, maybe buy some horses. Trout would like more animals, I think."

A small line crinkled her brow.

"Trout's my dog." As Prim made a small *o* with her mouth, I continued. "I rescued him about a year ago in a town outside of Shreveport. He was thin, jittery as a rattlesnake. I found him nosing around the dumpster behind a convenience store, sucking the meat off some discarded fish bones. Lucky I found him when I did, 'cause those things would've really messed him up if he'd swallowed them."

"Like rip a hole in his esophagus."

"Right." I rubbed my hand across the prickly sensation rising in my neck. I didn't like to think how things might have turned out for Trout if I hadn't found him.

"So I went inside the store, bought a couple cans of dog food, and used them to lure him away from the fish scraps. He followed me to my camper, and I gave him plenty of food and water—had a vet check him over the next day, too. Other than some intestinal worms and an ear infection, he was in fair shape. He's been with me ever since. He's not scared anymore, just spoiled rotten. Like a dog-bone-twice-a-week spoiled rotten."

"Trout…" Prim said his name with a hint of interest.

"Trout." I wasn't sure why, but I wanted her to understand how much I loved my dog, so I added, "The vet guessed he was about three years old—a lab and shepherd mix. I got him neutered and microchipped, too. Traveling around, I thought it was the safest thing to do."

Her lips curved into a smile. "For a guy who's lived his life with very few strings, Trout sure has grabbed hold of your heart."

I chuckled. "He's easy to like."

"Yeah, well, I think you're pretty easy to like, too."

"You should meet him." Jesus, this was getting personal…and risky. Sure, I wanted to spend more time with her. *But does she want to spend her time with me and my dog…?*

"Trout?"

I gave her a nod. *Fuck, please say yes, Prim. Just. Say.*

"I'd love to."

Jackpot.

Prim lifted her hands, and I pulled her to her feet.

With the steps to her advantage, she could look me straight in the eyes. And she did, without so much as a blink. "I want to ask you something, Chase."

Seeing as I was in no position to deny her anything, I said, "Shoot."

"What do you remember about that day you saved me from falling off the treehouse ladder?"

I rubbed my chin, scrolling through the years until I had the vision clear in my mind. Squirrelly little girl, spunky. Someone special, fragile, and steps away from trouble.

I cocked my head. "I spotted you from about twenty feet away, the backs of your legs, your feet in some old sneakers. You were shimmying down, and I knew one of the slats was loose, but I couldn't remember if Thorne had fixed it yet."

Prim bit her bottom lip, and I met her gaze, seeing something deep brewing behind her China-blue eyes.

"And I don't really know what happened next. I just had to get there, you know? Like Thorne wasn't there to protect you, but I was. I needed to be there when you came down to the ground. I just didn't think you'd drop ten feet into my arms."

She muffled a laugh then took a determined breath. "Do you remember anything else...?"

Prim was staring at my mouth like I'd forgotten something.

Something she hadn't.

A breeze pushed over her shoulder, and I breathed in the perfect Prim scent lifting off her skin. "Yeah. After I caught you and put you on the ground, I remember you had chocolate smeared right here." I touched her chin with my thumb, and it quivered just a bit. "You smelled like a cookie."

A smile crossed her lips. "Oatmeal chocolate chip."

Her ability to recall such a detail stunned me, intrigued me. I took a slow breath and let the memory of her small body in my arms return. Protectiveness rushed over me, and my tone deepened. "I also remember your face—God, it was white as a sheet. And you were shaking so bad."

"My heart was racing, but it was okay. I knew I was safe." She took my hand and brought it to her chest, and

I felt a rapid thumping beneath my palm. "Like I am right now."

"Prim—"

"Don't."

She closed her eyes, and I gazed at her cheeks. I don't think I'd ever paid attention to the softness of a woman's cheek before, or the gentle slope of her neck.

It was work *not* to notice Prim...or my hand resting on the swell of her round breast. It rose and fell with her rapid breathing, and when she finally opened her eyes, her irises were dark and wide.

"I'm not sure I'm okay to be with you like this." Her words carried a warning, but her tone hinted at raw need.

I took a step forward, sliding my hand to her nape. God, she smelled so good, and in that moment, I'd never wanted anything more than to kiss Prim. As my fingers slid into her silky hair, her breath came quick.

Remembering my promise to keep things PG, I brushed my lips against hers, soft and airy...until they weren't. *Soft and airy, I mean.* Electricity charged the air between us, and within a nanosecond, her body was pressed against mine, her tongue running over my lips.

Obviously, Prim isn't in the loop on the whole PG kissing thing.

I turned us slowly, leaning her up against the porch railing, and she curled her arms around my neck and deepened the kiss. She was an intoxicating mix of innocent and wild, tentative and provocative, and all I wanted was to have my fill of her.

"I always knew you'd be so fucking sweet," I murmured against her lips.

Judging by the way she fused her mouth to mine, tongue sliding and tasting, she liked a little dirty talk. I quickly hooked my arm under the leg she'd somehow wrapped around the back of my thigh. She plowed her fingers through my hair, sighing softly into my mouth, and suddenly all the soft curves and sweet friction flipped my caution light. Dangerously close to losing it, I broke the kiss and watched her gaze fall to my mouth. We were both breathing heavily, her eyes wide and lips flushed a deep crimson.

Prim cupped her cheeks. "Oh, God. I've gotta go."

What the fuck?

She wiggled out of my arms and darted up the stairs, then whipped around. "I had a really great time. Like, too great, I think." She dragged her hands through her hair, mussing it on both sides, before reaching into her purse. She dropped her keys—and a tube of lip gloss—before finally pushing the door open.

"At least let me check inside for—" The words died on my tongue as she ducked around the door. Before I could move, I heard the snick of the deadbolt and the scrape of the chain.

Her voice was muted, but clear. "Everything's fine, Chase. It's good. I'm good."

I took a step back and then another. I shoved my hands through my hair, stifling a groan. Well, I wasn't fucking good at all.

But this isn't about you.

I beat up on myself for a few more seconds, then took a deep breath and stepped into the line of the peep hole in the door. "Hey, it's okay. I'm good, too." I just had to believe she was looking at me from her side and added, "And it's all because of you."

I finished with a quiet good night and made my way to my truck. I drove home, grabbed a beer from the fridge, and dropped down on the couch.

Primrose.

I uncapped it and took a swig.

What the fuck.

I sat there, beer hovering at my lips, stomach tangled like a couple of fishing nets. Trout padded over to me, burrowing between my knees, and rested his head on my thigh.

I drummed my thumb on the bottle. "What's happening to me, boy?"

Coppery-brown eyes, wrinkled at the corners, looked up, silently urging.

This thing with Prim crossed the line of physical attraction. Sure, she was hot, but everything roaring inside me was about *her.* Intelligent conversation, expressive eyes, and purposeful hands—all catapulting me straight into an emotional landfill. And tonight, together under the stars, sweet pain had squeezed my heart.

I groaned long and hard over my beer. *Prim has me.*

I leaned back on the couch and stared at the ceiling beams.

Trout let out a mournful yowl.

Like she really *totally fucking has me.*

Chapter Eight

Saturday, August 13th 5:27 a.m.
Prim

I foraged through the box of cereal, pulling out the last cinnamon cluster and polishing it off. I wiped the sugar from the corners of my mouth and tossed the empty box on the table. *Why do I even* have *this in my pantry?* My sister would kill me if she saw me eating this garbage.

Goldie...

I glanced at the digital clock on my kitchen stove. *Fifteen minutes before I have to leave for the hospital.* I grabbed a chair at the table and tapped my phone on, needing my lifeline.

My sister answered on the second ring. "Hey. What's going on?"

In a voice knotted with hiccups and doubt, I pressed the speaker button and asked, "Am I anatomically and emotionally correct? Like, wired the way a normal woman should be?"

I heard the rustling of sheets and words spoken in a hushed tone to her husband but didn't have the grace to apologize for the early hour. The bonds of sisterhood didn't care about time.

"Please tell Max he's the most understanding husband on the planet."

I paused while Goldie relayed the message then I heard a door close. "Max says he loves you, too. But no worries. I'd be awake with Daniel soon enough." As a chair scraped in the background, I smiled, grateful my sister realized this was a sit-your-butt-down moment. "And the answer is yes. You're absolutely correct and normal."

Tension pulled at the back of my skull from a lack of sleep and an abundance of regret. Seven hours ago, I'd thrown myself at Chase. He gave me a sweet chaste kiss and I proceeded to shove my tongue in his mouth. "I'm not so sure. I think I send out little anti-man vibes."

"Impossible. You're the most thoughtful, intuitive person I know. Your vibes are fine—there's just a lot of deaf, dumb, and blind guys out there."

I chuckled despite my dilemma.

"Now spill, Prim. What's this really about?"

As I unloaded about the events of the past few days with Chase, I felt only marginally better with my messed-up feelings out in the open.

"You know this isn't about any stupid favor, right? Chase has gone way past whatever Thorne asked him to do. He legit wants to spend time with you."

I sighed, plowing through my thoughts. "But hear me out. I really do think it's some kind of signal I project, like I'm okay being single—my career and family and friends are enough. Some guys consider me a challenge, and they get into that for a while, but they lose interest soon enough. Most guys think I'm too serious, too predictable. Avery liked I fit into his mold—but it was just so messed up."

"The Ass was a cheater. Chase is nothing like that."

"He's been a player his whole life. What makes you

think he's suddenly changed?"

"Duh, he's not in his twenties anymore. Men grow up and learn to do better. So right now, with you, is his better."

I shook my head. "No way. It's the hunt he's after. Chase loves the chase."

"Come again?"

"Nothing." I blew a wisp of hair from my forehead. "It's just something I overheard him say. In high school."

My sister groaned. "Good Lord, can you give the guy a break? It was *high* school. Enough said."

"It's not like I'm opposed to a hookup. Who knows? Might be the best thing to ever happen to me."

"As long as it's what both of you want, and you're open about it."

I leaned forward, crossing my arms on the counter. "I mean, I'm on the pill. We'd use condoms."

"Already smarter than me."

"Yeah, but your relationship with Max was completely different. He was never a player, and he made his intentions clear. You getting pregnant wasn't planned, but it was good." I release a long-suffering sigh. "Why did Thorne have to come up with this crazy idea anyway?"

"You really don't see it, do you?"

I tucked a loose strand of hair behind my ear and hunched over my phone. Goldie had a flair for the dramatic. The only thing missing was the drumroll.

"Listen to me. Is it true our brother stuck his nose where it didn't belong? Yes. Absolutely. No surprise there." As her kettle whistled, she said, "Wait. Gimme a sec."

I heard the tap of a teacup on the counter, then my

sister returned. "But seriously, Prim. Chase is a grown man, free to make his own choices, and he's *choosing* to hang out with you. It's totally clear he's into you. Chase Bova is—"

So out of my league, a tiny voice filled in.

"—Holy shit. *Chase. Bova.* Initials C.B." Goldie sucked in a breath. "He's the one, isn't he? From that journal you kept when we were kids?"

I could deny it, but what was the point? I covered my eyes, sighing. "The same."

I filled her in on my hopeless teenage infatuation with Chase, from the treehouse to high school to last night's tongue-jousting. When I finished, my heart actually felt a little less cagey. Liberated. *And maybe even a little hopeful.*

"Oh. My God. It's destiny. An honest-to-goodness *real* love story. Like the song."

"*No*," I said, ignoring her.

"*Yes.*" Goldie urged. "The treehouse is your balcony, and he's your prince."

"You mean, Romeo."

"Whatever." She sipped her tea noisily before continuing. "The point is, she loves him, and he loves her, and they live happily ever after."

My chin dropped. "But they die in the end, Goldie."

"Nope. Not in the song, they don't."

Inwardly, I winced. "Fine. But either way, falling in love requires two willing people, and with my toxic vibe, my guess is Chase is in it for the challenge. He wants to crack the nerdy kid sister code."

"Ugh, enough already. You're stalling...with all these ridiculous notions about *vibes* and *signals*."

Elbows on the counter, I rested my chin in my

hands. "You know you sound like Mom."

My sister laughed. "Good. Now, listen to this question, because it's what Mom asked me when I was all wigged out about Max."

I chewed the corner of my lip.

"What do you hope to gain by not telling Chase about your true feelings?"

Flip a pancake. It took a moment for my brain to get from start to finish—to avoid any detours—before I landed on a definitive, "What the hell, Goldie."

She laughed. "Yeah, that's pretty much what I told Mom…minus the H word. But I didn't get off that easy and neither are you."

"Okay…" I blew out air from my cheeks. "Honestly? I just don't want my heart to get broken again. A rejection from Chase would crush me. Absolutely crush what little self-respect I have left. I couldn't survive that."

Her sigh reverberated through the phone. "Fair. I get it. Then, maybe you should step back and regroup. But whatever you do, please put a stop to this *thing* you two have going on. It's too messy. How can you find your true Mr. Right with Chase in the picture?"

Her words echoed my thoughts. Chase filled my dreams, and now with him popping up in my life, there was nowhere to hide. *I don't like hiding.* Fear about watching a horror movie was one thing. But fear about letting the greatest guy in the world slip through my fingers was another.

Fear sucks.

"No." I swallowed hard.

My sister gulped, sputtering. "What…?"

I waited a few beats before continuing, reaffirming.

"I said *no*. I'm tired of waiting in line and never getting my turn."

"Uh-huh. Doing what everyone *thinks* you should do, instead of what you *want* to do."

"I know you know what I'm talking about."

"Yep. Been there, done that."

I glanced at the clock, shaking off the fact I should've left for work five minutes ago, and asked one more question. "Be honest with me, Goldie. Am I crazy…?"

"Yes. Absolutely. But you're also an anatomically, emotionally correct woman. Your wiring's in amazing shape. I say go get your love story. It's about damn time."

****

I continued to mull over my conversation with Goldie as I worked my shift. I thanked God it was a light day—a broken wrist, food poisoning, and a case of walking pneumonia—and after treating the patients, we sent them all safely on their way.

I thought about heading to the pool after work, but since the idea of swimming alone felt tedious, I settled for a shower. While the mix of steam and soap made nice with my muscles, it did little to clear my emotional brain fog. Afterward, I changed into my leggings and sweatshirt, toed into my flops, and headed home.

As I pulled into the driveway, my stomach lurched with the parking brake. Chase was sitting on my porch step, phone in his hand and a dog's head resting on his foot. He waved at me.

Flip a stack of pancakes!

I climbed out of my car, hugging my bag to my body. "Hey, Chase!" I silently winced at my way too cheery voice, hoping he hadn't noticed.

Chase stood, a smile lighting his face. "Prim, I'd like you to meet Trout." He rubbed behind his dog's furry ear with one hand and gestured toward me with the other. "Trout, this is Prim. You know, the girl I've been telling you about?" Trout let out an engaging bark, and I was hooked—*literally*—by the gentle dog named for a fish.

I dropped to my knees and ran my fingers through his soft coat. Looking into his eyes, I crooned, "Hey, Trout. Aren't you a good boy, such a sweet boy." When his tongue lapped my cheek, I laughed. I lifted my gaze to Chase. "He's so friendly."

"That's because he knows I like you…and he never questions my taste."

"Blindly trusting, huh?"

"Exactly." Chase winked, shrugging his backpack higher on his shoulder, and the clanking had my head tilting. He jiggled it again for emphasis. "Your kitchen sink, remember…?"

Awareness hopscotched across my heart. He'd promised to fix it, and here he was, waiting on my doorstep. I stood up, finding the grace to blush. "Thank you."

My gaze drifted to Chase, dressed in a T-shirt that clung to hard muscles and fell loose at the waist of his jeans. Even the scuffs on his work boots had scuffs, and the hole at his knee teased a sexy bit of skin. Though he owned the rugged tool-guy look, it was his kind protective nature splashing warmth in my body. Wave after wave of it. And I melted a teensy bit on the inside.

I shuffled my feet. Chase had kissed me in this very spot last night. And I kissed him back. Then I'd left him in the dark.

Way to show him you're not that dorky kid anymore.

I tucked a strand of hair behind my ear and worried my bottom lip. "If I'd known you were coming, I'd have made something for supper."

"Which is why I didn't want to say anything."

"Wait. Has Thorne been talking about my cooking?" My hands fell to my hips. "About that stupid sweet potato casserole?"

He covered his mouth to hide a laugh. "There's nothing stupid about sweet potato casserole, Prim. But no. He didn't say anything. I just didn't want you to go to the trouble of cooking. You've been at work all day— you deserve a rest." He tipped his head to the bag hanging on his other shoulder. "I've got supper covered."

I blinked a few times while waiting for Chase to vanish into thin air. Because that's what dreams did— and so by default, dream guys had to do the same thing, right...?

Only he didn't disappear, fade, or even go fuzzy for a moment.

I took a step forward, and my next thought tumbled out of my mouth. "This is the nicest thing any guy has ever done for me."

"Remind me to have a talk with Ace and Thorne and Sage."

"Brothers aren't guys."

Chase nodded, brushing his finger under my chin. "Then clearly you've been spending too much time with assholes."

A giggle bubbled out of my mouth, but thankfully I stopped short of snorting. Chase was right, of course. When I was a girl, I believed in thoughtful, charming princes like my brothers, Ace, who took out the trash,

Thorne, who did his own laundry, and Sage, who washed dishes. But sadly, grown-up Prim hadn't discovered a single guy worthy of a crown.

Well, other than you...

As the moment stretched between us, Chase smiled, soft creases framing the corners of his eyes. *This is nice.* The kind of nice I could get used to. But before I tripped down that black hole, I gathered my wits and led him inside.

True to his word, Chase had my kitchen sink running like new within the hour. We found a survival series on streaming and dug into supper—an Italian sub and a pint of potato salad. With a couple beers in hand, things were humming along quietly between us and the nomads in backwoods Alaska.

"So, what happened last night?" Chase asked, putting the TV on mute.

Until they weren't.

I'd hoped I wouldn't have to get into all of that. Surely the crew that'd just nailed a deer and trapped a couple of squirrels in the tundra made for better conversation than my sex-crazed tree-climbing antics.

His eyes narrowed, and my resolve waffled. He wasn't going to let this go. There was no point in prolonging my embarrassment. He'd been nothing but nice, and he deserved an answer.

I could smack myself in the head for ever going along with my brother's ridiculous idea. Maybe I'd needed a somebody to get me out of my relationship funk. But did that somebody have to be so magnetic and irresistible...and my teenage fantasy?

Talking about it isn't going to be easy.

Chapter Nine

Saturday, August 13th 8:55 p.m.
Chase

"Talking about it will make it easier." I looked at the adorably confused expression coloring Prim's cheeks and nudged her with my knee. "I'm a good listener."

A smile cracked her lips, and something tight and small twisted inside me. I really wasn't a good listener, and I never had been. Basically, I steered clear of anyone and anything that forced me into my feels. But for the first time in my life, I wanted to listen…to Prim.

She hesitated for a few seconds, and when she finally scooted back on the sofa, resting her head on her arm, my insides unwound a little.

"You probably think I'm some silly female."

"More like a sexy female."

She laughed down at her beer. "Probably because I tried to climb you like a tree last night."

"What is it about you and me and trees anyway?" I took a swig then added, "Let me just say you *climbing* a tree felt a hell of a lot better than you falling out of one."

Her cheeks pinked, and she shifted, tucking her feet beneath her. "Like what's wrong with me…?" She swung her gaze to the TV, as if studying the soundless screen for hidden clues, worrying her bottom lip between her teeth. "Thorne thinks I've been having a rough time with dating, but it's way worse than that." Her gaze fell on me. "I totally suck at it."

I crossed my arms over my chest. "No way. Last night was perfect."

"Until I freaked out on you." She pressed her fingers to her temples. "I don't even know what came over me."

Prim's voice squeaked in the most adorable way imaginable, tripping a wire inside me. Hands down, when it came to men, she was as clueless as she was beautiful. I had to admire her tenderness and the way she took things so seriously.

As I took in my next breath, air zigzagged through my lungs. I'd been climbed by plenty of aggressive she-bears in my life and walked away unscathed. *This is so different.* Prim had scaled me like a sleek little mink raiding a bird's nest.

And she's clueless as fuck what she does to me.

I shook my head, grabbing hold of my composure. "You didn't freak me out. I'm an easygoing guy, and I don't spook easily. But I have to tell you it pisses me off the guys you've been with have been such jerks." I pulled on my beer then tipped it toward her. "Then again, if they weren't, I wouldn't be here with you."

A little smile curved her lips, and she tentatively met my gaze. "I mean, it's not like I planned on being alone in my thirties. I knew I was a late bloomer. When I didn't have a date at all in high school, I told myself I'd meet my guy in college. My plan was to reinvent myself—keep the good grades part but make more friends, join a sorority. Be fun and flirty."

She paused between sips then continued. "After graduation, I figured I'd probably meet Mr. Right at the hospital. You know, a cute nerdy lab tech who liked to talk data—maybe a sleep-deprived resident hungry for a hot meal and a listening ear." She shrugged. "Maybe that's part of the problem. Too much thinking and figuring and planning."

She closed with a weighty sigh, and I flipped into fixer-upper mode. "Planning's overrated. The point is to be in the present, so you don't miss the good stuff. Mother Nature doesn't plan shit. You can't plan a rainbow."

"True." She tilted her head. "But what about monarch butterflies…?"

Their migration? I dragged my hand over my jaw, feeling the stubble of my evening shadow. It prickled, a little like her question, but I liked her sharp mind. It kept me on my toes.

"They do follow a cycle, a path. You can mark your calendar by them." I pointed my beer in her direction, countering. "But not the northern lights."

"The aurora borealis?"

As she shifted, focusing like a dog pointing on a bird, I inched closer, lowering my voice. "Sure, they have forecasts for the aurora, but it's notoriously hard to plan for."

Prim gathered her hair in her hand and draped it over her shoulder. The tips of it brushed her breast, and my thoughts coasted south of my waistline. I watched her raise her bottle to her mouth. As her lips curved around the opening, I remembered her thirsty kisses from last night. *Drugging kisses.* As she released the bottle, her lips made a soft sucking pop, triggering a twitch inside my jeans.

"And what about the cycle of salmon spawning?" she asked, a hint of sassy in her voice.

I raised my eyebrows. I didn't see this on my bingo card. Leave it to Prim to pose a question to a fisherman…about *fish*.

God, her mind is so fucking hot.

"Another naturally occurring cyclical phenomenon." As I spotted the twinkle in her eyes, I caved to the smile pulling at my mouth and raised my beer to her in a salute. "Okay, so maybe Mother Nature *does* plan some of her shit."

Prim clapped her hand over her mouth. I felt like I'd just reeled in a prize game fish, making this sweet girl laugh. It made me wonder what it'd feel like to make her moan.

"Yeah, she does." She put her beer on the coffee table then took my hand. "Thanks. You have this way of making me feel better."

As a laid-back guy, I got this compliment a lot. Only I hadn't expected it from her. Possessiveness I had no right to feel surged through my veins.

I locked my fingers with hers. "I like taking care of you."

There was a beat of silence, then she withdrew her hand and reached for the remote.

"Don't." I gazed into her blue eyes, and seeing no rising storm clouds, slid closer. I put my beer on the table beside hers and reclaimed her hand.

"Want to know what I've learned about you?" When she tried to squint past me, I gently lifted her chin. "You don't give your affection away so easily." She shook her head, but her gaze never left mine. "And I think you've had good reasons not to."

Uncertainty rippled her expression. "Would you believe Boyfriend Number One told me I was missing a libido?"

"A fucking idiot."

She shifted, sitting up straighter. "Guy Two called me a nosy bitch when I suggested his online betting looked more like an addiction than a hobby." I pulled my brows together, and she added, "Yeah, one time I was going down on him and he actually checked his phone—started cursing at the screen." She dropped my hand to push the sleeves of her sweatshirt up past her elbows. "The jerk was lucky all I did was leave the room."

I lifted my chin. "You should've left your mark on him, if you know what I mean."

She laughed a little. "Then there was Number Three, a narcissistic asshole married to his fraternity brothers. Our relationship ended pretty fast. I met my fourth boyfriend after graduation. He was decent enough, but after a few months, when he suggested I get a breast augmentation—and offered to pay for it and a vacation to the Bahamas to christen my hot new boobs—I bailed."

This has to be the dick Thorne told me about.

"Just for the record, your boobs? They're perfect." She blinked her long lashes at me, and I added an unapologetic, "Yeah, I've noticed. A few times."

My admission brought a smile to her face, but it quickly faded. She tucked her hair behind her ear. "And I don't want to talk about my last boyfriend."

I stand corrected.

My curiosity spiked, but while I wanted to know how Number Five had out-dicked his predecessors, I let the silence pulse between us. Wait time was think time. No different than when I went to be alone on the water, waiting for a fish to bite.

Prim pushed out a heavy breath. "I thought he loved

me. Like we'd talked about marriage, how many kids we wanted, what style home to buy in Saint James Park."

My brain stumbled on the "kids" part—easily my least favorite subject—but I recovered quickly. "That's a high-dollar Raleigh neighborhood."

She bit her lip and nodded. "My other boyfriends had their issues, but it didn't seem to matter so much because I never loved them. They didn't hurt me, you know? But Avery did."

I ran my hand across the heat rising at the back of my neck. "Any guy named Avery has to be a prick."

She shoved her hand through her hair, pulling it through to the ends. "Looking back, I see there were signs all around me. He used to brag about manipulating loopholes and fudging client billings—"

Great. A professional jerk.

"—and then there was the time he took credit for the gorgeous demi-cuff bracelet *I* bought for us to give his sister on her birthday."

She curled her hands into little fists. "Oh and get this. His name's Avery Smith-Stanton. I should've cut and run the minute I realized his initials spelled the word 'ass.'"

For a few prideful seconds, I basked in the knowledge this guy had lived up to his name, leaving Prim for me. Then a creepy crawler feeling swarmed across my shoulders, and I knew I was better than that. Her feelings had been real, and she'd gotten hurt. I gazed down at her hands, glad they were no longer fisted, hoping her feelings for the guy didn't run too deep.

"He showed his true colors about five months into the relationship, when I swapped shifts with another nurse so she could attend her nephew's bar mitzvah. I went by his condo with some fresh seafood for a surprise supper and noticed his office door ajar."

Shit.

"I heard Avery before I saw him. I figured he either had some really good porn going on his laptop or he was jerking off. But the closer I got to the door, I knew something was up. He didn't make those kinds of sounds when I touched him." The blue of her eyes darkened. "I found him kicked back in his chair, a head bobbing between his thighs."

"Fuck her, Prim."

"Fuck *him*, you mean."

I winced.

"I know, right?" She looked away. "But gender wasn't the issue here. Cheating is cheating. Avery cheated on me, something I don't think the other four ever did." She swallowed, blinking back to my face. "So, was catching him on the verge of an orgasm with someone else really such a shocker?"

"You do understand this wasn't about you, right?" I bent so I was level with her face. "Cheaters are battling their own demons. Insecurity or lies…or some other bullshit that's made them unable to be honest with themselves or anyone else. He was in the wrong."

"Maybe. But I still think I'm romantically stunted." Prim pulled her feet beneath her and knotted her hands. "Like there's something wrong with me—like I send out invisible anti-man vibes. Or that I'm not sexy enough. Or that my lady bits don't work the way they should."

I shook my head, pretty sure these were the most pathetic statements I'd ever heard from a woman. I studied the brave curve of her jaw. I swore under my breath, instantly wanting to protect her from every selfish prick she'd ever known. This was Prim. *My Prim.*

As I watched a tear pull on her lashes, a cold lump of anger settled in my gut. I cocked my head and waited, mentally coaxing her to meet my gaze.

Prim swung her legs around and dropped her feet on the floor, pushing herself up. She scrubbed her hands over her face and finally looked down at me. "It's okay, Chase. Really. I'm fine."

****

Prim

I grabbed our empty beer bottles and burned a path to the kitchen trash can. I felt Chase and his larger-than-life presence following me, but I still made my way over to the sink. Trout stopped at my foot, looking first at Chase then at me. With a snap of his fingers, the dog dropped to the floor.

Chase moved in from behind, wrapping his arms around me. "Don't be afraid. I'm not gonna let you fall." His breath brushed warm against my ear. "I've got you."

I turned around inside the circle of his arms, only briefly surprised when I looked up to his profile blocking out the overhead light. I inhaled, and his scent of fresh cotton became the security blanket I desperately needed.

I shook my head, so weary of feeling like an emotional ambulance, and pushed back the panic squeezing my chest. "Sex. It's okay, I guess. But in my experience, it's mostly about the guy coming. No man has ever made me come." Confusion clouded his gaze, so I clarified, because if I was going to put this out there, I needed it to be factually correct. "No, that's not exactly true. No man *in the flesh* has ever made me come."

Chase chewed on the inside of his cheek for a moment, then opened his mouth and quickly closed it.

"Shit, shit, shit." I mumbled, tilting my head back and staring at the water stain coloring one corner of the ceiling.

"Look at me, Prim."

And I did, groaning like a teenager.

"Jesus." His gravelly voice made me lean back on my hands, tilting away from him. He was about as mentally collected as me…which wasn't saying much.

He shoved his hands through his hair and hooked them around his neck, making his underarm muscles pull tight against his shirt. "I'm trying to understand—like *really* fucking understand. But you've got to help me out here."

With his plea, reality swarmed over me, unlocking a decade of pent up doubt and frustration. Emboldened, I hopped onto the countertop and waited until I had his gaze. His gentle-giant brown eyes narrowed, and I readied my nurse's tone—the one I saved for patients who needed facts.

"What I'm saying is no man has ever given me an orgasm—not with his fingers or his mouth or his penis. Sex doesn't work for me. I'm the only one who takes care of me…well, me, my vibrator, and a really good fantasy."

He leaned toward me. "I said it before. You've been with the wrong men." Before I could form a reply, he brushed my cheek with his fingers then moved a strand of hair off my face. "Tell me what you imagine when you touch yourself."

The fact he phrased this as a command and not a question sent tiny tremors through my body, all of which settled deep in my belly. I squeezed my eyes shut and shook my head from side to side because sharing my secret was too much.

"I want you to stop shaking your head."

My initial reaction was subdued shock. The floor creaked as he stepped forward, then I felt his hands cover mine, his thumbs rubbing tiny circles on my wrists. And we stayed like that for a series of long intimate seconds.

"Good." When my eyelids fluttered, he added, "No. Keep your eyes closed. And breathe, babe."

The snake-charmer quality of his voice calmed my pulse, and with more breaths of silence connecting us, I felt my body slipping into a trance.

"Now," he said in an even beat. "Tell me what you imagine when you make yourself come."

With his sensual command, my back arched involuntarily, and a sigh hummed in my throat. *God, you know how to use your words.* I wiggled my butt, transforming the laminate countertop into the cozy velvet pillows inside a genie's bottle. But even as warmth bloomed beneath my skin, I wondered how I could possibly share my most intimate secret with *him.*

I let my head loll backward, and on my next breath, Chase's scent pirouetted through me, bringing reality to my fantasy. In my mind, I saw windblown hair flecked with streaks of afternoon sun and eyes the color of cognac. Slowly, his image took shape, fuzzy edges morphing into the hard lines and flat planes of his shirtless torso. Tan skin marked with soft blond hair met my gaze. As my vision expanded, so did the muscles laddering his stomach. A daunting shield tattoo flexed on his bicep, begging for my touch.

I wiggled my left hand free from his grip and traced a path up his arm with my fingertips. I didn't need my eyes. I knew exactly where to find his ink. I gently rubbed it, and hearing the low hiss of his breath, my lady bits tingled.

Oh my God, how can I not tell him?

"Him," I said, clinging to a tiny thread of courage. "I imagine *Him*."

****

Chase

Sex—consensual and always practiced safe—lived at the top of my priorities. But this moment with Prim, witnessing her dormant sexuality come to life, was beyond hot. I couldn't remember ever being this turned on.

I'd never cared about a woman's sexual past. History was irrelevant when my goal was getting naked in the present. But then I'd never let myself think about a woman the way I did Prim. In a matter of weeks, she'd invaded my senses, making me question why I slept with women I didn't love.

As she squeezed my bicep, my breath hissed. *I'm going to right your sexual history. Reset it, make my mark and claim it.*

I searched for a tone to match my resolve and tilted her chin up. "Open your eyes."

Prim blinked, and I captured her gaze. I couldn't help myself. I needed to understand her confession. My voice dropped an octave. "*Him...?*"

As a blush rose from the curve of her neck to her cheeks, one sweet word sliced through the air. "*Him.*"

Blood hammered between my ears, anticipation rising between us. Was it insanity to hope I was part of her fantasies? Who was I kidding? *I want to star in them.*

Prim lowered her gaze, eyelashes flat against her skin. She hugged her arms around her middle, then ran her hands up her stomach to cup her breasts. "Sometimes I imagine him kissing these." As she palmed the perfect mounds, my jeans grew tight. "And I can tell by the way he draws teasing circles over them with his tongue, he likes them."

"He more than likes them." I barely recognized the sandpaper edge of my voice.

With her bottom lip wedged between her teeth, she slowly raised her head and released her breasts. Her eyes grew wide with dawning, understanding she controlled the narrative of her sexuality.

Instinctively, I rubbed the ridge at the front of my jeans. I'd never been so hard in my life. When her gaze followed my hand, irises darkening to a smoky blue, damn if my inner caveman didn't beat his chest. One corner of my mouth turned up. "Do you do this to *him*?"

Prim nodded, rubbing her palms on her thighs. "And when he goes down between these—"

"Lucky bastard."

"—he lets me play with his hair."

"Is his hair straight or curly?"

After what felt like an hour of seconds, she gave me a quiet, "Straight. And thick."

Thank fuck.

Prim dipped her hands lower, to the snug V between her legs, until her fingers disappeared. "I like to run my hands through his hair while he moves his lips over me...*here*...and slips his tongue inside me."

Holy...

Prim shifted, pressing her thighs together. Tiny bolts of energy charged the air, dissolving her vulnerability and threatening my sanity.

"Sometimes he's naked and I go down on him, only

117

in my dreams I do it so well there's never any doubt he enjoyed it." Her gaze drifted across the room then came back to me. "Or he presses me against a wall, and I hook my legs around his waist."

God.

"Who, Prim?" I pressed my forehead to her chin, inhaling her scent. "Who. Is. *Him?*"

As she swallowed, I glimpsed the perfect ripple of her throat. Her breath fluttered, and her fingernails scraped the countertop. "I think you already know."

I lifted my head, all but growling against her lips. "Fuck."

I parted her legs, wedging myself between the juncture of her thighs, grabbing her ass and pulling her against me. I kissed her, our tongues tangling and teasing, trying to connect more deeply. I wished I could sink through her smooth skin and make a home for myself in her silky essence.

I pulled back for a moment, letting the sheen of perspiration on her neck and sweet flush of her skin draw me in. Prim was more than a sexy beautiful woman. Her mind amazed me, her heart lassoed my every emotion, and her body…? *It fucking owns me.*

My hands slid from her waist up her sides, stopping to cup her breasts. I'd caressed many in my life—some crafted by God and others by a surgeon—but none had felt so…*right*. As I brushed my thumbs over her nipples, she gasped and leaned her head back.

Invitation accepted.

I kissed along her collarbone and spoke against her skin. "You're perfect, Prim." I pulled her sweatshirt over her head and trailed my tongue over the gentle swell of her breasts. "From this moment on, no one goes here but me." I kissed her nipple concealed behind her sports bra and felt her heartbeat drumming beneath my lips. I slid my hand over to where hers hid between her legs. "Or here." Gazing at her emotion-stained face, I chose my next words carefully. "I take care of what matters to me. *You* matter to me."

I kissed her, parting her lips and nipping her plump bottom lip. She met my urgency with her own, and I deepened the kiss. Desire pumped through my veins, a storm surging, pushing, testing my limits. Prim dug her fingers into my shoulders, sealing her body against mine.

I pulled back, cupping her chin, brushing her cheeks with my thumbs. "God knows I love a good fantasy, but I'm here, Prim. *In the flesh.* I want to make you come."

****

Prim

With one look into Chase's sin-dark eyes, my pulse tripled, and the truth spilled out of my mouth before I could even think of stopping it. "God, yes."

In one fluid movement, he dragged my sports bra over my head. His gaze touched my eyes, my lips, then moved lower to my breasts, lingering there, consuming me. As he thumbed my nipples to pebbled points, he leaned forward, teeth scraping the shell of my ear. "Do you know how hot you are?" Nothing but a squeak of air passed my lips, and he cupped me in his hands. "I want to kiss these."

He blazed a path with his mouth down my throat to my breasts. As he drew one nipple into his mouth, teasing it with his teeth, hunger pooled between my legs. With each slow pull of his lips, my breath came quicker. *Flip a fucking pancake, he knows how to use his mouth.* I closed my eyes and let my hands find their way into his hair.

He growl-hummed his approval, teeth scraping, his husky voice warm against my skin. "I think I can make you come just like this."

I moaned as he swirled his tongue over the tip, drawing and pulling. My hips began to move in searching seeking circles against the buttons on his fly. He clutched my ass with his hands, bringing us closer. Heat spread from my core, throbbing and needy, and my thighs trembled.

"Fuck." He spoke against the pebbled point, gritty and raw. "That's it. Give me one."

My back arched involuntarily, and my head fell back. Tiny sparkles burst behind my eyelids, my fingernails digging into his shoulders. He wrapped me inside his arms, holding me so close barely a breath separated us. He rubbed tiny circles over the small of my back with his thumbs, kissing the soft skin behind my ear. As my body and mind slowly returned, I sighed. A long, delirious sigh like I'd never heard before.

Chase felt me through my leggings. "Is this me?"

I nodded.

As he tugged at my waistband, I braced my hands on the counter and lifted my hips. He moved with a determination that matched the long hard bulge behind the fly of his jeans, stripping me out of my remaining clothes and carrying me to the table. He kissed me, teasingly and achingly slow.

"I want to kiss you." His words brushed against my lips.

"You are," I said, giggling and tugging his shirt up his torso. Our lips parted long enough for me to pull it over his head and toss it on the floor. I rubbed my palms over his furry chest and let my gaze follow the line of hair down his laddered stomach where it disappeared below the waist of his jeans.

Chase lifted my chin, kissing me again and gently parting my thighs. "Here." His hands ghosted higher, and I sucked in a tight breath. "I want to kiss you here."

Realization dawned, amplifying the nerves pulsing through my body. Chase had just given me a skyrocketing orgasm with only his mouth on my breasts. How could I possibly survive one *there*? Even while pleasure flickered from where he was lightly stroking me, another thought seized me.

"Chase."

"Hmm?" His lips vibrated against my neck.

"I don't know if I can. What if I can't…"

He slid his finger between my folds, then lifted it to my lips. "I know you said this is me. But it's also you. And you are very responsive." He eased me back, kissing a path over one breast, past my navel and lower. Moonlight filtered in through the lace kitchen curtains casting a filigree pattern on the ceiling.

"Hands, Prim."

I lifted my head, slowly melting at the sight of him between my legs.

"I want you to play with my hair." He pressed an open-mouthed kiss right *there*, then added, "While you give me another one."

Needing his touch more than anything else in the universe, I shifted toward him. As I weaved my fingers through his hair, his lips moved over me, claiming me, consuming me.

And I knew I'd never ever be the same.

Because Chase Bova…you are my universe.

Chapter Ten

One Week Later
Saturday, August 20th 1:10 pm
Chase

I stared at the sunlight skipping over Cormac River and the crowd of kids—and Prim—splashing and playing around its banks. I truly loved being around children, talking and hanging out with them.

As long as they aren't my own...

Thank God I'd had Grandpa's salty-dog sex talks to plant my feet on the straight and narrow when I was a teenager. When it came to safety, I was a good foot soldier, following his advice so I didn't get saddled with a kid or some nasty disease. As I watched a couple of boys playing tag by the water, I blew out my breath in my hands.

Jesus.

Kids.

My kids...?

I shook my head, cementing my resolve. There was nothing between today and someday that would result in the world seeing another Curt or Chase Bova. *Nothing.*

But because I still loved kids and wanted to build on the success of our Lake Michigan excursion with the boys in Green Bay, I'd started researching similar opportunities in North Carolina. Turned out McClendon

House, a private facility associated with our local foster care system, welcomed community partnerships. I'd read their report card—mostly healthy children, two mental health counselors on staff—and hoped with some time and days like today, we might bring a little fun into their lives.

I'd been looking forward to getting out on the water with the McClendon kids, dubbing it a blend of charity and homecoming. I'd grown up in Vista Falls, and after steering clear from the place my entire adult life, I felt like I was defying the odds being back and feeling so damn good about it.

Renovating Grandpa's house.

Connecting with my sister and niece.

Creating and collecting memories with Prim.

I drew my gaze from Prim and adjusted my baseball cap, feeling pretty damn sure one lifetime with her wasn't going to be enough. *Not even close.* Trout made a circle and sat on his haunches, looking at me. I scratched behind his ears, then patted his back. "No worries, buddy. I got this."

After a morning shower had cleared—and with earthy smells of dirt and plants hanging in the air—my crew and I rafted with the kids down river. Next we took the path to Huggins Cove, a beautiful spot where water tumbled over rocks and greenery draped over stone-covered bluffs. Then we fished and sifted through creek beds, and now, with all of us secluded in a cluster of oak trees, it was feeding time.

In the week since that incredible evening Prim and I spent together, we'd continued seeing each other. We swam laps in the evenings, and afterward made out in my truck with our hair still damp. I took her out to dinner and the movies on her night off, barely making it back to her place without ripping her clothes off. Yesterday, we played fetch with Trout in the dog park, then I brought her over to my house. We had supper from the grill, then I went down on her for dessert.

Being with Prim was intense, yet so far we'd only had oral sex.

Only.

A paradoxical word because every lick, nip, and kiss had rocked my core. And since I'd never had sex without a condom, I found it equally disturbing how much I wanted her bare, skin to skin. After all, she was on the pill.

I blew out a breath, convinced whenever I finally found myself buried inside her—God help me, bare—I might spontaneously combust.

Sometimes Prim and I didn't do anything but talk and kiss—a strange new world for me because I'd never kissed a woman without hoping it'd lead to sex.

I rubbed my hands up and down my thighs, belatedly remembering to breathe.

But lately, I'd caught myself fantasizing about Prim, about kissing her for hours. Earth-shaking kissing—the kind where doing anything else seemed unnecessary. I didn't even know if that kind of kissing existed, but somehow I imagined it could with Prim. Still unsure how I felt about these thoughts invading my headspace, I was beginning to understand what my sister said about a woman driving a man crazy.

In the distance, I heard the screech of a car's hatchback lifting followed by some victory clapping.

"Oh, yeah. Chocolate chip. Come to Phil."

I stole a look over my shoulder just in time to catch

Phil, my Chase n' Dreams cameraman, salivating over a tower of cookie boxes. Given he was five foot ten and an even one hundred sixty pounds, where he hid the pounds of food he ate every day remained a mystery.

"Give me those," Phil's girlfriend said, hip-bumping him and covering the boxes with her arms. "You can have all you want after the kids eat." She planted a conciliatory kiss on Phil, and he reciprocated. Enthusiastically.

A little too enthusiastically.

My gaze cut across the picnic area at the dozen kids and Chase n' Dreams crew members scattered everywhere. I wiped my hand over my face, groaning inwardly. "Get a room, would you?"

The couple managed to separate, then laughing, made their way over to the picnic tables. They added the cookies to the spread of hotdogs, apples, and bags of chips.

I adjusted my sunglasses, my gaze settling on Prim sitting at a table, braiding my niece's hair. The sound of their laughter carried through the air, and when Prim finished weaving the pink ribbon through her hair, Charlotte sprinted over to me.

"Look, Uncle Chase!" She twirled around, holding a braid in each hand. "Aren't they pretty?"

I opened my arm, and Prim slid into place, fitting her body to mine. I felt her gaze on my cheek, and my fingers found their way to the soft skin at her nape. "Charlotte, those are the prettiest braids I've ever seen."

She tilted her head to one side. "Even prettier than Aunt Prim's?"

With that question, my niece lit a Roman candle in my body, firing it up like the Fourth of July.

Prim sucked in an audible breath, her fingers digging into my side. "Oh, Charlotte. Sweetie, I'm not your—"

"Yep. Even prettier than *Aunt Prim's*." I swung my gaze from my niece to Prim, watching naked emotion flush her lovely face. "Although I have to admit," I added, giving her long blonde braid a reassuring tug, "I've been a fan of your braids for a long time. Since you were just about Charlotte's age."

That got a giggle out of Charlotte.

"No way. Wait." After a few seconds, Prim's eyes lit up, and her tone softened. "Really…?"

I laughed and hushed back, "Oh, yeah. But don't let it go to your head or anything."

Rather enjoying the stunned look on Prim's face, I took my girls' hands and led them over to the food. We ate with all the kids, listening to their stories told with ketchup spots on their chins and cookie crumbs stuck in the corners of their mouths.

At one point, Prim brushed her thigh against mine and looked at me. Her skin was soft and smooth, and the scent of her—coconut sunscreen mixed with soap—unraveled me from the inside out.

Prim smiled around the rim of her water bottle. "Hey, you."

"Hey," I said, just as soft.

She squeezed my hand under the table. "You okay?"

Other than the fact I'm running a marathon of the heart on a lifetime of one-night sprints…?

"Absolutely."

Her gaze did a circuit of my face. "Have I mentioned it's a really wonderful thing you've done here today?"

"I just hope the kids had a good time."

"Look at them, Chase." She squeezed my hand again. "Really. Just *look*."

When I did, I saw a collection of hotdog-and-cookie-stuffed faces. Their clothes weren't spotless, but they were clean. Their tennis shoes were practical rather than trendy. I straightened, sorting through my thoughts. The memory of wanting the cool brand of jeans in middle school no longer stung, but it lingered. I made a mental note to sponsor a Christmas shopping trip for these kids—to get things they not only needed, but really wanted.

I met Prim's gaze and gave her a self-deprecating smile. "It was the fishing. Or maybe all the cookies."

Charlotte climbed onto my lap, and several more kids followed, and before we knew what was happening, we were a human clump of laughter.

Prim leaned over and kissed my cheek. "Or maybe it's all you."

****

Prim

I'd just slipped into my pajamas, snuggling under a fleece blanket on the sofa, when my phone dinged. I glanced at the screen, and my toes curled.

Was it crazy I'd come to expect texts from Chase? I loved how he sent me little snippets of his day. Just a few words with a picture of him with an assortment of screwdrivers at the hardware store, or a shot of Trout in a life jacket perched at the bow of his fishing boat. He often sent them while I was at work, and I wouldn't see them for hours. Somehow, I liked those even more…

We'd spent the day together with the kids on the river, each agreeing we were exhausted. Secretly, I was a little disappointed he didn't invite me over, but I understood the need for space.

I reached for my phone and swiped it open.

—What are you doing?—

I looked at the glass dangling between my fingers, then set it aside and typed.

—Just got out of the shower. Lying on the sofa now. Having a second glass of wine.—

—Damn. I like this picture.—

He added a red-hot flame emoji, and I giggled.

—What'd you do after you showered?—

—Put on my pajamas.—

—OK. And before that?—

My eyebrows crinkled. I'd dried off, combed my hair, and put on some lotion. When I replied as much, he replied with the yawn emoji.

I twirled my finger around a strand of hair, lip wedged in one corner of my mouth. Before I could think of something flirty, he texted back.

—Use your words. Paint a picture for me. Like one of your songs.—

I dropped my phone on the sofa, shoved the blanket to my feet, and looked down my body. I rubbed my calves together and watched my toes curl. The lace edging of my shorts and cami lay flat against my skin. As I slid my hands up and down my thighs, a decidedly breathy sound escaped my lips. Moments later, smiling, I reached for my phone.

—I sat on the edge of the bathtub, sipping wine and massaging vanilla body butter over my skin. Then I piled my hair in a messy bun and slipped into my pajamas.—

—That's good. Now give me some suspense.—

Chase was a man used to giving orders, and the way he gave directions made my skin tingle in all the best places. Suspense was the slow ache building between my legs. I reached for my wine and took a long deep swallow. My fingers shook as I typed.

—*I wish you could see them. Tight pink boy shorts, elastic waistband, with a matching lace trim cami.*—

—*Better. Now take me to the best part of the song.*—

I pulled the blanket over my body, drawing my knees up to my chin. I closed my eyes for a string of seconds, then opened them, peering down at the lace strap hugging my shoulder. As my fingers tapped on the screen, my breathing picked up. Then I pressed send.

—*I like it when you bite the elastic with your teeth. And it snaps against my hip. My breath hisses when you fist my cami in your hands.*—

It took barely a heartbeat for him to reply.

—*And your panties?*—

I paused, thumbs hovering over the screen, then typed two little words.

—*What panties?*—

I waited for the little dots to pop up, and when they didn't, I slid my free hand under my thigh.

—*Sorry. TMI.*—

I saw the little dots, then they vanished. Only to appear again…and disappear. *Now you've done it.*

—*No way. You were kidding today, right? That you sucked at sexting?*—

My mouth lifted into a smile. I shifted on the sofa, squeezing my legs together, his words lighting a match inside my body.

—*Never done it much. But I think I like it with you. Will you paint me a picture now?*—

—*Okay. Yeah. Just give me a sec.*—

My legs were visibly shaking, my gaze glued to my

phone screen. The dots were there for the longest time…until they weren't.

—I dreamed about you last night. It was dark, a fire burning in the fireplace. You were wearing nothing but my shirt, and I could see the outline of your nipples in the light of the flames. When I peeled it off your body, and you were naked in front of me, all I could think was how it'd feel to be inside you. Buried. Deep. Safe.—

Flip an effing pancake. I'd bitten my lip so hard I felt the indentation when I ran my tongue over it. I gulped down what remained in my glass.

—I may need more wine.—

—Haha. It's a sexy game. idk it feels different with you.—

I swallowed past my uncertainty.

—Different good or different bad?—

—Good. But it scares the hell outta me.—

The dots flashed for a second, then this appeared.

—Because I want more.—

Sexting…? The question sounded loud between my ears. The warmth rising in my neck had to have me looking as pink as my pajamas.

—More what?—

The dots were there for a while. Beneath the blanket, my feet tapped on the sofa. I stared at the phone in my hand, willing it to light up, whispering, *please, please, please…*

—You. More of you. Fuck, I want all of you.—

I sucked in a breath, feeling stunned, antsy, practically euphoric. I typed madly.

—Can you come over?—

He tagged back a thumbs-up, and I scrambled to my feet, tossing the blanket to the floor.

****

I heard a bark at the door, then footsteps. I flipped the latch and let Trout dart through my legs before launching myself into Chase's arms. God, he smelled good, and burying my face in his neck, I breathed him in. We'd gone from sexting to vulnerable admission in just fifteen minutes. While adrenaline surged through my body, panic fluttered in my stomach. I wasn't sure he realized the power he held over me. If things went badly, he'd leave my heart split open like butterfly shrimp.

"That was fast," I whispered against his shoulder.

"Like that day I saw you climbing down from The Hideout. I couldn't get to you fast enough."

I tilted my head. "I'd say your timing has never been better."

"God, I hope so."

And here I thought I was the only one with nerves. I ruffled my fingers through his hair, choosing my words carefully.

"You know everything about me, Chase—my past, my hopes, my fantasies, all of it. And we've been fooling around, and it's been the best time of my life." I lifted my head and gazed into his dark brown eyes. "But if we do this, you should know it means something to me. It means *everything*."

Chase pulled a paper out of his pocket and handed it to me. I unfolded it, reading his name and the date—less than a week ago—and the test results listed in a chart.

I blinked, understanding consuming me. "You did this for me?"

"I want you to trust me. This seemed like a good place to start."

"I got checked, too. After Avery. I'm clean."

A smile tipped the corners of his mouth. "You're clean all right. So pure. And insanely smart and sweet. Funny, and generous to a fault." He pulled my bottom lip into a kiss, then spoke over it. "And so damn sexy."

He took a step back and slid his gaze down my front. He dropped to his knees, rubbing his hands over the backs of my thighs and biting my elastic waistband. When it snapped against my skin, he gazed up at me. I expected to see his dimple deep in a smile, a kind of masculine satisfaction marking his expression.

I cupped his cheeks. "What's wrong…?"

Several heavy moments passed before he pressed a kiss on my palm. "Everything with you is a first for me. Every laugh, every touch." He stood, steadying me when my feet shuffled awkwardly. "When I close my eyes, I see these soft wisps of hair right here." He brushed his fingers over my forehead. "How they frame your face so perfectly, same as when you were ten years old. Or sixteen."

I shook my head. "You never looked my way, Chase. Even though you did with lots of other girls." I crossed my arms, his test results in my hand. An ugly memory bubbled to the surface. "Remember the time you wandered into the girl's locker room, wearing sunglasses and tapping a yard stick on the floor?"

"Pretending to be a blind man wasn't one of my better moments." The cringe in his voice was palpable.

"Allison Murray flat-out dropped her towel. God, she had the biggest boobs." My gaze fell to my lackluster chest, then lifted. "The rest of us couldn't get out of there fast enough. And we all knew what was happening when she skipped her next class."

He scratched his head. "I didn't know you had gym

with her."

"Yeah, well. I did."

I looked away, wondering why I was plowing through this muck, into a past where he'd never given me so much as a passing glance. *Because I need to know what's changed.*

"It's no secret I've thought with my dick for much of my life. But it's not like that anymore. I'm thirty-four, and as sad as this is gonna sound, I've never been in love."

With the L-word, a meteor shower burst inside my chest.

"I think that means I was patient, Prim. Waiting for you to come into my life."

As silence squeezed the air between us, I shifted my feet. "Maybe…or it might just mean you're mental."

He touched my arm with feathery strokes of his fingers. "That's fair. You're definitely in my head. You're all I think about."

"But why now, why *me*?"

As Chase took me in his arms, awareness rushed through me. Warm inside this man blanket, there was no hiding what he did to me. I tingled where his fingers touched the bare skin above my "not sexy" elastic waistband.

He loosened his arms, dipping his head to look in my eyes. "I think you're hugging my heart."

My chin dropped.

"It's something Carrie told me, about how the right woman would steal my breath and hug my heart and shit." He drew me closer and pressed his lips to my forehead. "I don't know what I'm doing. I get sex. But with you, it's different."

I turned so my breath brushed his cheek. "I keep waiting for you to walk out of my life."

"I can't. I'm in too deep." He looked at me from beneath lowered lids. "But I probably should. You're incredible, Prim. You deserve a better man than me."

I shook my head. "Why would you say that? You, you're amazing."

Chase gave me a one-shoulder shrug. "I put on a pretty good show but trust me. I'm a little broken inside."

His admission tripped in my head like a clock striking midnight. Façades. Personas. We all had them. An image we projected to the world that when examined closely, revealed cracks around the edges. Knowing how humans were all a little broken, the last thing I wanted was to fixate on the cracks. *His or mine.*

We stared at each other, an eternity passing in a few seconds. As a shiver wiggled up my spine, his arms tightened around me. I had no doubt if I got spooked and asked him to leave, he'd kiss my cheek and politely walk away. I wondered if he knew how his thoughtful attention, how his willingness to hand over the steering wheel, made me feel secure and safe.

I want to give you the same.

"Have you forgotten I'm a nurse?" I asked, watching his Adam's apple bob with a heavy swallow. Desire felt like a pent up breath I couldn't hold onto any longer. "I have lots of experience with broken. I've got healing hands, you know."

"You think you could put them to work on me?"

"Absolutely." Pressed against him, I could feel the button on his jeans through my cami. I slid my hands lower, unfastening it. "You're like sex on legs, Chase Bova. I've got a fix for you."

"Keep talking dirty, and you'll never get rid of me." He kissed me, moving his lips over mine, demanding. He seared me with his warmth and something deeper, stronger.

Yearning.

"I want to make love to you so much." He dropped his forehead to my temple, whispering over my ear. "But only if you're ready. More than anything, I want to get this right."

I placed my hands on his chest and kissed his cheek, his forehead, his lips. I felt his heartbeat galloping beneath my palms, reminding me I wasn't the only one with a stake in what happened tonight. Though our approaches were vastly different, we'd both skirted the boundaries of risk and vulnerability for far too long.

I met his patient gaze, speaking without hesitation. "God, yes. Please make love to me."

My lips brushed his, and I felt light and hazy, dreamy. As he lifted me with his hands, I wrapped my legs around his waist. He deepened the kiss, and we melted into each other. Instantly lost.

Miraculously found.

****

Chase

I took Prim to her room and gently lowered her to her feet. I indulged, flicking that elastic waistband again, digging my fingers in the softness of her cami before sliding them both from her body. I took a step backward, unable to drag my gaze from her soft curves, so beautiful in the moonlight. For me, there was no one else.

And there never will be.

I shed my clothes and met her on the bed, covering her in kisses. Light ones over her calf, and an open-mouthed one to the scar on her knee. I trailed my lips over her hipbone, past her navel, and up to her breast. My tongue teased her nipple, awakening it, and my hand drifted lower to that most secret part of her, finding the rhythm that matched my mouth.

The sound of fingernails scraping sheets filled my ears, and I gazed up at her, lip wedged between her teeth, head tipped back on the pillow. I loved how expressive she'd become with her body these past weeks. Some moments later, as her breaths came faster, a soft moan escaped her mouth. She cried my name, arching her back, trembling. The sight of her, so pure and sensual, made my heart buck like a bronco trapped in a corral.

I held her close, caressing her skin, waiting until she came back to me before crawling up her body and fitting my hips between hers. I placed my arms on either side of her head and whispered into her ear. "Should I get a condom?"

She shook her head. "I'm on the pill."

I lifted a silent prayer of thanks and steadied my breath. As the idea of being completely joined with Prim took shape, a collision of possessiveness and urgency overtook me.

I groaned through the sweet torture, somehow managing a hoarse, "And you're sure? I promise, we can still stop." I honestly didn't know how I could, but I would. I'd swallow glass for this woman.

She ran her hands through my hair, rubbing her fingers over my neck. "I love you for saying that, but I'm sure." Her mouth twitched into a sexy smile. "I want you."

I held her gaze and slid into her with gentle thrusts, inch by careful inch. God, she was so tight I had to fight to keep control. When we finally became one, I could see the realization—of what we were doing, of what this meant—glimmering in her eyes. I bent my head, kissing her with soft slow strokes of lips and tongue. She kissed me back, and nothing could have prepared me for this flawless, seamless, endless connection.

"You okay?" My voice dragged thick and heavy.

"I'm perfect."

Yes. Yes, you are. I kissed her again, not caring we were talking about different things, because for the first time in my life, I got it. I finally understood what my sister meant about the ass-knocking and breath-stealing.

As I began to move inside her, she ran her hands over my chest and wrapped them around my neck. I gazed down at this sweet, beautiful woman beneath me. For most of my life, I'd been about as fixed and secure as a sky full of storm clouds. But not anymore.

Prim anchors me.

She met my every thrust, her eyes wide and dark. I watched her mouth part on a sigh, and reading the intensity of her breathing, I shifted my hips, giving her what she needed. I waited for the moment when her voice hitched, her thighs trembled, and her body bowed off the bed. As she gasped, I moved with her, prolonging her pleasure, loving how it flushed her cheeks.

And then I followed her, spine itching, hips jerking, hungry with my need for her. Somewhere in the haze of it all, I felt her arms around my neck, fingernails digging into my flesh and snipping the last thread of my self-control. A groan ripped from inside me, and I came long and hard, convinced the earth had shifted with the force of it.

I breathed heavily into her soft skin where shoulder

met neck, and I knew—joined like this with her—I was home.

Prim is home.

I kissed her, and her warmth seeped through my skin. My movements shifted to lazy and loose, delirious with her softness beneath me. Her hands entwined around my neck, and just as my thoughts began to float, I heard her say, "Let's stay like this forever."

Still inside her, I held my weight on my arms and claimed her mouth, giving my senses over to the magic of her lips. Was it possible to fall so fast? It was as if once I'd allowed myself a drink, I knew I'd never leave the well. She restored me.

Maybe, just maybe, I restore her, too.

"Then let's do it. I want to be with you more than anything." Emotion thickened my voice. "I've never felt like this, Prim. You're absolutely the most important person to me. I don't want to be apart from you. Not ever."

Her eyes widened. "I-I'm a little afraid."

"So am I." I pulled her bottom lip between mine, gently nipping. "But hey, I think it's okay as long as we're both a little afraid together."

She smiled, and I moved inside her, already needing her again. As she lifted her hips, meeting me where we were joined, a fresh ocean of want washed over me.

She kissed her way across my throat, speaking against my flesh. "Just in case you can't tell, I'm falling in love with you."

Instinctively, I jerked her closer to my body. No woman had ever said that to me, and I wasn't prepared for just how perfect it sounded coming from Prim. It was relief and pressure, thrill and dread, shaking like maracas inside my head.

Maybe I am completely mental…

I shoved my thoughts away and brought my lips to hers. *So soft. So sweet.* As she deepened the kiss, her hug around my heart tightened. Slowly, I thrust inside her, seeking her warmth and shelter.

I leaned into the sensations, my feelings, and whispered over the shell of her ear. "Thank God. Because I'm already in love with you."

Chapter Eleven

Three Weeks Later
Saturday, September 10th 4:30 p.m.
Chase

I placed the basket on the shelf by the bathtub and thumbed through the contents one last time. I'd been Special Agent Bova for the past week, uncovering clues as to how to best stock it with all of Prim's favorites: sleeves of little round cotton pads, a package of silky glide razors, sensitive-skin shaving cream, shea body butter, no-show antiperspirant, a soft-bristle compact head toothbrush, anti-plaque toothpaste, and mouthwash. I filled the linen closet with new white bath towels and enough washcloths for her to use a fresh one every day for two weeks before laundering. Overkill? *Probably.* Wishful thinking? *I hope to hell not.*

Prim arrived at my place after work, ponytail sagging, barrettes askew, and sweat stains under her armpits. As I wiped specks of mascara from her cheek, I gave myself a mental high five for grabbing a pack of makeup remover wipes in the checkout line.

I led her into the bathroom and made a sweeping motion with my hand. "You should stay over."

And she did.

****

Prim

As days drifted to weeks, and weeks to a month, our relationship grew, evolved. Between outings to the hardware store for remodeling supplies and swimming laps in the pool, a blueprint of Chase Bova took shape in my mind. Beneath dimples and smiles lived a man driven to succeed, restoring his home and redefining his purpose.

Utterly laying claim to my heart.

This morning, I lingered in bed, but not because Chase was still with me. He'd slipped away earlier to do a promotional sequence with a local boat and RV dealer. I burrowed under the sheets, smushing my nose in his pillow, and inhaled. Sweet, sexy, musky man tickled my senses, and I figured life couldn't get much better than this.

Our connection flowed almost effortlessly. We talked every day, and I'd gotten a lot better with the whole sexting thing. And sex was intense—sometimes flirty and teasing, sometimes urgent, but always tender and intimate. We made each other laugh, and at night with our heads on the pillows, we talked about everything.

And that's the very best part.

I stretched my arms over my head and rolled out of bed, patting Trout's head before padding over to the bathroom. Rubbing the sleep from my eyes, I came up short at my basket sitting empty on the countertop. My gaze fell to the three open drawers on the left side of the cabinet. Sneaking a look inside, I found my things in neat rows inside the top two. I chewed on my finger for a moment, then caught my reflection—and something scribbled—on the mirror.

Let's live together.

I ran my finger over the white shaving cream letters, stopping at the heart shape dot over the letter 'i'. I leaned closer, then took two steps back, squinting. I used to heart that letter—and exclamation points—the same way when I was a kid. Did he know that? Was it just a coincidence…?

I read the words again, then dashed to the bedroom, grabbed my phone, and swiped my favorites.

"Hey. You left yet?" I listened, tapping my foot on the floor. "Anyone there? Mom, Ace…?" I chewed on my bottom lip, ruffling Trout's furry neck. "Good. I'll be there in twenty."

****

I made it to Three Creeks with five minutes to spare and flopped down on the sectional. I snuggled with my nephew and buried my head against his neck, simply breathing him in. Daniel smelled like vanilla pudding, chicken sausage, and warmth, and if I could, I'd curl up with him in my arms and never move again.

Goldie's voice lifted from the kitchen. "My little man woke me up at one thirty and then again at four. I feel like a glob of limp noodles." She walked toward me with mugs in each hand. "How Mom did this six times remains my greatest unsolved mystery."

I nodded my agreement. Our mom, a retired high school English teacher with an endless supply of poetry and bandages, was the G.O.A.T as a parent. And she'd had to fly solo when Dad passed away. When it came to motherhood, Mom left Amazon-sized shoes to fill, but Goldie was finding her own stride. And I was so proud of her.

"Poor little guy. Teething sucks, huh?" I kissed Daniel's forehead and settled him on my lap. "Sorry you're running on fumes, but if it wasn't for him, you'd be gone already. I'm glad, like *really* glad you're here."

Goldie set my mug on the table, then blew over the top of hers. "And why does this feel like an intervention?"

Her observation slammed me. Was that what this was? I needed saving now, before I got in deeper, unable to survive another botched relationship?

"Maybe because it is?" Tucking the baby safely in the crook of my arm, I fished my phone out of my pocket. I pulled up the picture I took before I left Chase's house.

"Or maybe it's more of a crossroads. Definitely a serious leap of faith." I turned my phone around, showing her, and her chin dropped all codfish-like. "Yep, that's the message Chase left me this morning—on the bathroom mirror. Oh, oh, and swipe to the next picture. Check out the cabinet." Goldie leaned in, looking from the phone to me then back. "Yeah, he opened all the drawers on one side of the vanity and put my things inside. *For me.*"

"Holy crap, Prim."

"I know, right?" I met my sister's gaze. "Like what the hell do I do?"

"You listen to your heart."

"Flip a pancake." I pressed my palm to my forehead. "You make it sound so easy. Thorne's gonna shit—"

"Don't worry about him. He's back to being Professor Vreeland."

"I'm not so sure about that. He went to Portland for something."

She sputtered into her cup. "Wait, what...? Like Maine?"

"Nope. Oregon."

"What's he doing now? Restoring a redwood cabin?"

I laughed, then quieted. "Who knows? Says it's something for a client." *But I don't buy it.*

"Well, whatever." Goldie sipped her tea. "Thorne will be fine. Have you forgotten Chase is his oldest friend?"

"No, I haven't forgotten, but there's also Mom. What will she think?" As I ticked through my mental list of family, uncertainty bloomed. "And what about you and Billie? I mean, I'm your big sister, and I shouldn't be living with some guy. And God knows what Ace—"

"Honey, he's not just some guy." Goldie covered my hand, effectively cutting off my verbal vomit. "We all just want you to be happy. It's easy to see you're in love with him."

I groaned. "Is it that obvious?" She nodded. "But Chase could hurt me so bad."

"He could also be your perfect match."

My sister came in for a hug, sandwiching her son between us. His sweet little glurps and fuzzles filled the air, and my thoughts leapfrogged.

To *our* bathroom cabinets.

To *our* mismatched dinner plates and glasses.

To photos of us together—ones we hadn't even taken yet—sprinkled around *our* den.

I bent my head to kiss Daniel's hair, breathing him in.

Moments later, my sister covered Daniel's ears with her hands and whispered, "Crossroads, my ass. It's a leap of destiny!"

Chapter Twelve

The farmhouse smelled like caramel apples, buttered popcorn, and apple cider. Voices hummed all around me, and I instantly felt warm, snug, encircled in something that didn't exist in the world of the planned and driven. I glanced at Chase as he dumped another bag of chocolate bars in the pumpkin-shaped bowl.

It only exists with Chase and my family.

Suddenly, the screen door squeaked, feet shuffled behind me, and the gaggle of geese known as my family fell silent. I whizzed around, brushing elbows with Chase.

"Hey! Happy Halloween everybody." Thorne stepped into the kitchen, a small child dressed in a bandana and overalls in his arms. His can't-forget-you smile glowed with something new, unexpected, *real*. He held his breath for a few moments, then on a gusty breath said, "I want you all to meet Jacob. My son."

Except for the voices coming from the den TV, stunned silence zinged through the room, until Billie's daughter, Chloe, with legs crossed, announced, "I have to go potty, Mommy. And I can't get my ladybug costume off.'"

As Billie led her daughter to the bathroom, she gaped a did-you-know-about-this look at me. I shook my head, thoughts ricocheting through my brain. Thorne, my big brother—the bellwether barometer of the family, my meddlesome but well-intentioned protector—had a *son*. It was all I could do not to crane my neck around Thorne, in search of the boy's mother.

Mom moved first, dragging her hands through a kitchen towel and crossing the length of the room. She rose on her toes, kissing Thorne's cheek repeatedly, then gathered both of them in a hug. I shelved my questions for later, knowing in this moment, nothing mattered more than welcoming the newest little farmer Vreeland into the family.

When Mom pulled back, her eyes glistened.

Thorne hugged his son closer and kissed the tufts of blond hair curling around his blue bandana. "I think he looks a little like me."

"No, he looks a lot like you...and Dad." Ace clapped him on the back, and as my mom took Jacob into her arms, my big brothers shared their own embrace.

My heart swelled with so much love it was hard to breathe.

"What the fuck?" Chase mumbled, his words sucker punching my heart. I felt his body lurch forward when his sister elbowed him in the gut.

"Language please, little brother," Carrie said between clinched teeth.

Chase looked at her, then Thorne, and as almost an afterthought, his gaze swung around to me.

"What...?" I mouthed, eyes narrowed.

Clouds marked his expression, and as the rest of my

family descended on Thorne, Chase lifted his chin in a nod, half smiled, and gave me a gentle nudge. "It's okay. You go on ahead."

****

Chase

And that's how things rolled for the next few hours.

We ate corn dogs and caramel popcorn with Chloe and Charlotte.

We munched on candy.

We made the kids something called "green monster" punch, and the grownups drank cold beer. *Well, Ace and I did anyway.*

And with a kid-friendly Halloween movie playing on TV for Chloe and Charlotte, we listened as Thorne described the winding tale that led him to his little boy.

Three years ago, Thorne had a summer fling with a visiting professor in the humanities department. Though he and Jenna texted some after she returned to Oregon, she eventually ghosted him.

In March of this year, as Jenna was pulling out of a hidden driveway, a utility truck hit her car, killing her instantly. Heartbroken, her mom took custody of Jacob, but with her advancing Parkinson's disease, there was no way she could manage caring for a toddler. Once Jenna's will made it through probate, the woman contacted Thorne.

Now, I sat on the couch, watching my best friend sprawled on the floor with the kids, his son tucked within the bend of his long legs. Sure, Jacob clapped when he caught a rolling ball, and he had oatmeal cream pie smeared on his overalls like your everyday kid. But when I studied him closely, squatting like a frog by Thorne's knee, my shoulders grew tight. As Jacob's quiet gaze roamed the room, measuring our faces with quiet concentration, I saw a bit of myself.

A short time later, Prim began reading a story to the girls, and I made my way outside for some fresh air. I went straight for the garage, lifting the lid on the crate beside the garbage can and pulling out a tennis ball. I tossed it between my hands a couple times before throwing it against the wall.

Bing. Bang. Slap.

I caught the ball with one hand, then pivoted and paced across the concrete driveway. I'd always been that guy whose brain worked best when his body was moving—some kind of zen between my left brain and right brain. I never questioned it much, just accepted the fact I processed things differently than other people.

Bing. Bang. Slap.

But there was no way I'd been the only person in the room thinking, "what the fuck." I was just the only one with guts enough to say it out loud.

Bing. Bang. Slap.

I ran my thumb over the grooves of the tennis ball. None of this shit made any sense.

Bing. Bang. Slap.

Thorne, a dad…?

Come on, fatherhood for guys like us made about as much sense as people wanting flying cars. Sounded great, but really…? With as many bad drivers as there were on the ground, why the hell would anyone want that in the sky?

Bing. Bang. Slap.

The door swung open, and hoots and cheers carried from the den to outside. As Thorne walked toward me, he spared a glance over his shoulder. "Billie's really on a roll with the trivia game."

"Impressive since your mom's the best player in the family."

"Yeah, English teachers know a little bit about a lot of shit." He glanced at me sidelong. "But I think I stumped her today."

"You stumped the whole damn room."

Thorne rocked back on his heels. "Sorry, but there was no way around it. I wasn't sure what would happen once I got to Portland. Jenna's death stunned me, but finding out about Jacob?" His breath caught on his son's name. "I was fucking blindsided, you know?"

I nodded and wondered for a moment how I might have reacted if someone I'd slept with presented me with a kid. Would I have bolted? Would I have dialed in to some hidden sense of responsibility that sometimes sex dealt serious consequences?

I didn't have to wonder for long.

"I know we were only together for a few months, but I cared for Jenna a lot. Sometimes we talked about the future, but nothing specific. Nothing binding. Then she just dropped off the grid—not a call or even a text to say we were done. I blamed it on long distance and bad timing, but I'm kicking myself now. I should've known better."

"What, are you saying you would've married her?"

He crossed his arms and lowered his head. "I honestly don't know. She took that choice from me, and I can't figure out why."

Thorne lifted his gaze, searching my eyes, and I felt a tiny chink forming in my armor.

"What did I do to make Jenna pull away from me, to keep me in the dark about my own child? I must be a complete asshole." He clipped his words roughly, then shook his head. "So anyway. That's why I couldn't talk about Jacob to you or anyone. Not until I went through all the paperwork, until I was sure."

"And are you…? Absolutely sure?" I blurted, regretting the blunt accusation in my tone.

Determination creased his brow. "I did my homework. Jacob's mine."

"And what are you gonna do with a kid?"

"My son, you mean," he said, scratching his neck then allowing a slow grin to inch up his face. "I dunno. I've got so many ideas running around in my head, I can't decide what to do first. But mostly I just want to love and protect him. Reassure him that he means everything to me."

I shook my head. "For someone who used to line up his Army men in formation on his bedroom shelf, you're taking this change really well."

He crossed his arms over his chest. "What are you getting at?"

"I'm saying this kid—"

Thorne sliced a glare at me, and I squeezed the tennis ball between my hands, taking in a pair of measured breaths. "Jesus. I just meant your *son* is gonna wrinkle the shit out of your life."

"I'm a pressed shirt, Chase. Not fucking *starched*." He waved his hands, palms open. "And what would you have done if you were in my shoes?"

"For starters, I wouldn't have gotten in your shoes in the first damn place."

"Says the guy who screwed more girls in high school than I have in my entire life."

"Well, apparently you missed the lesson my grandpa

gave me." Reading his crinkled brow, I added, " 'Cover your wanger before you bang her.' "

Thorne chuckled painfully, dropping into a patio chair and leaning forward, arms on his thighs. We verbally shoved back and forth a few more times, then a rumble of thunder sounded in the distance.

I tossed the ball between my hands, then looked at Thorne. "I guess you've always had a soft spot for strays."

"I took you in, didn't I?"

"Asshole."

He clasped his hands in a fist between his knees, looked away for a moment, then turned back to me. "Look. You and me, we've always been straight with each other. You know you can say anything to me, and I won't give a shit. But I won't let you call my son a stray."

I nodded, then threw the tennis ball on the wall.

Bing. Bang. Slap.

I wasn't sure why, but I rocketed the ball through the air once more.

Bing. Bang. Slap.

"I know it sucks your dad never stepped up," Thorne began.

Ah, yes. Here it comes.

"Especially after your mom passed, Curt should've been there for his children."

I'm reminded even Thorne Vreeland is sometimes either crazy or stupid.

"You and Carrie deserved better. It wasn't fair, and I've always hated that for you."

Yeah? Want to know what I hate?

I hated pity.

Bing.

I hated being different.

Bang.

I hated me.

Slap.

Catching the ball, I froze, railing against the envy seeping into my bloodstream. *I'm better than this.*

"It's hard to explain. Jacob's a part of me—the best part of me. He's my responsibility. But more than anything, I feel like he's a blessing."

"That sounds really…" My voice came out hoarse, and I cleared my throat. "Nice."

Thorne pushed up from the chair. "Yeah, it's nice…until everything turns fucking scary. Half the time I don't even know if I'm doing anything right."

My grip on the ball tightened for a moment, then it relaxed. This was Thorne, my best friend. Prim's brother, for Christ's sake.

I exhaled a long breath. "Take it from a guy who knows. Just be there for Jacob. Stand by his side. And never let a day go by without telling him you love him."

"Chase. I didn't—"

I held up my hand. "Don't. I'm here for you. Enough said."

"You know I'd do the same for you." Thorne sucked in a breath and almost as an afterthought added, "But it wouldn't be anything like this for you and Prim."

I barked a laugh. "You got that right. You'll never catch me in this situation."

He scratched his head. "Abstinence is the only sure thing, and I know *that's* not you. What makes you think you'll never be father of the year? Are you shooting blanks?" He stepped toward me. "Shit. Did you get the cut?"

"No, I didn't get *the cut.*" I snorted, but for a split second his question made me think maybe my swimmers lacked some gusto. I'd used condoms religiously, but even they weren't one hundred percent effective.

This is bullshit.

"I've just always used condoms, okay?" *Except with your sister. Because being skin-on-skin with her is fucking phenomenal.* I shook my head, then tossed the tennis ball up in the air and caught it with one hand. "Didn't want to get saddled with a kid."

"Until you're ready, right?" He grabbed my arm. "You do want a family of your own someday, don't you?"

I looked past Thorne's shoulder, into the nothingness of the night sky. As thunder rolled again, my neck grew warm, prickly.

"Jesus, Chase." He blew out his cheeks, walked off, then spun around on his heel. His eyes narrowed. "What exactly are you doing with my sister?"

I challenged his gaze. "Getting to know her. Spending time with her and—"

"You're living with her," he said, voice fuming. "And don't tell me you've told Prim how you feel about kids, because if you had, I'd know about it."

"We haven't had the conversation, no." I lifted my chin in defiance. "But believe me when I say this. Prim doesn't tell you everything."

Thorne planted his fists on his hips. "Why did you come back anyway? I love Vista Falls and this farm, but it doesn't mean I want to live here again."

"That's because you've made a successful life for yourself in Atlanta. And now you have a little boy who's depending on you. But me?" I said, tone sharp. "I haven't made a home anywhere. This is all I've got."

But even now—with Prim, Trout, and Grandpa's house—I wasn't sure I had the grit to make it a real homeplace. Refinishing hardwood floors and installing new faucets were cosmetics. The jury was out on whether my foundation was truly sound.

He rubbed his chin. "Well, I'm wondering if it isn't just a pit stop until you get the itch to roam again."

His comment crawled over my skin. It reminded me of a certain race car mechanic and his excuses.

Even though Thorne was my oldest friend, I'd never confided in him about Curt. As a kid, I hid my feelings of abandonment. As an adult, anger and embarrassment kept me from talking to him—or anyone—about that November night in a Las Vegas casino. I didn't know what that said about me, other than I was a fucking Houdini when it came to evading my feelings.

Thorne had no idea how hard Novembers were for me.

And it's almost November again...

"I'm not a flight risk, okay? I'm here because I want to make Vista Falls my home." I threw the tennis ball.

Bing. Bang. Slap.

"But even if I did take to the road again, Prim could come with me."

Laughing, he turned and walked a circle around the driveway.

You don't know her as well as you think. I wanted to tell him about her dream of being a traveling nurse, about her songwriting…but they weren't my stories to tell.

Thorne came around and stopped in front of me. "Enough of this bullshit. Let's talk facts. You're living with my sister. You've never been in a serious relationship. She loves you. You're not being honest with her." He hesitated, teeth clenched. "You're going to destroy her."

"I love Prim. She knows that. Now, do I need to talk to her about some things? Sure. Yes. And I will."

He cupped his hands over his mouth and blew out a long slow breath. "She'll give in to you—take whatever scraps you're willing to toss at her. Is that what you want? Is that how you show her you love her? By making her choose between having you and the prospect of never being a mother?"

I turned, palming the tennis ball in my hand before releasing it.

Thorne lunged, snatching the ball on the bounce. He walked away and dropped it in the chest.

He returned with a look of warning. "Jesus, Chase. Please. Rethink this, for Prim's sake. And if you can't…" His voice faltered. "Then you have to let her go."

"Go where?" Prim asked, popping out of the shadows. She held Jacob in her arms, and the vision twisted my gut like a pretzel.

Like we'd done our whole lives, Thorne and I exchanged a secret look, only now we weren't buddies covering for each other about staying out past curfew.

Right now, the stakes were higher. *So much fucking higher.*

I knew Prim wanted to be a mother, was made to be one. But I needed him to give me time to figure this out.

Shifting, I reached for Prim's hand. "I was just telling Thorne about…a trip I've gotta make soon. To Texas."

Prim tilted her head, hoisting Jacob higher on her hip. "Texas?"

"Yeah, and he—well, we *both*—think you should go with me. We could watch the migration." A hundred needles pricked my neck. It wasn't exactly a lie. I'd been thinking about taking her there in the spring, because it was pretty much too late to see them now. Only she didn't know their pattern.

Or at least I hope she doesn't.

"Monarch butterflies…?"

I breathed in the crisp night air, but it was tainted with the bullshit spewing out of my mouth. "Absolutely. Just you and me and some of Mother Nature's planning."

With a barely concealed frown, Thorne walked over to Prim and lifted his son in his arms. "I think there's a storm coming, so I'm gonna go. It's way past Jacob's bedtime anyway." He turned to me. "Think about what I said. You should really let her go."

Prim glanced between me and Thorne. "I mean, if you know when you're going, I could definitely ask off work."

"Let's talk about it when we get home."

I turned, locked gazes with Thorne for a few moments, then rubbed his son on the back. "Good night, little guy."

Jacob looked at me—*straight* past my bullshit—and resting his head on his dad's chest, popped his thumb in his mouth.

As I watched them leave, Prim slid her arm around my waist. I pulled her closer, kissing the top of her head, thinking tonight would be my last with her.

And then, it began to rain.

Chapter Thirteen

Monday, October 31st 7:45 p.m.
Prim

"I'm broken, Prim. I've always known it. You just made me forget for a while."

There was a reason why I'd never strapped a bungee cord around any part of my body. Maybe I was adrenaline-deficient, but somehow I'd always had the good sense to steer clear of possible doom.

Until Chase Bova.

I listened as the rain thumped on the roof and rushed down the gutters. Trout perched on his bed by the fireplace, but his ears perked up with our words. His protective canine instincts sensed the tension between us, so thick you could slice it and serve it on a platter, and his dark eyes followed our movements.

I looked from the dog to Chase, blinking back traitorous tears. "You may be broken, but you're not beyond repair. You're still living with the pain, grieving, and you think you're not worthy of love. You're still angry with the father who abandoned you."

"No," he said, way too quickly, covering, deflecting.

"You are." I touched his cheek, feeling it quiver beneath my fingers.

He removed my hand, breaking our connection. "Don't, Prim."

Our gazes locked. Anger pushed up inside me and forced its way out. "Funny. I never took you for a coward."

Chase turned away, and that's when I knew the depth of his hurt. *Like Grand Canyon deep.* Teeth clenched, he moved past me, grabbing a simple black picture frame and taking it apart. He thumbed through the photos until he landed on one.

Clutching it in a shaky hand, he closed the space between us. "Look. See that guy? That's my dad. Curt. Bova." He pushed out a series of antsy breaths. "Notice anything...?"

I did, and awareness raised the fine hairs on my arms. I'd never met Curt Bova or even seen a picture of him. Until now. I hedged and said, "Not exactly."

"You're a terrible liar." He slid the photo in my line of vision, voice challenging. "Look at him and then tell me *that* guy isn't standing right here in this room with you."

"Don't be ridiculous. You're not your father."

Chase shook his head, a harsh laugh ripping from someplace deep inside him, and tossed the old photograph on the coffee table.

I put my hands on my hips. "So, you look like him. That doesn't mean a damn thing."

"But it does. It totally fucking does. I'm also restless like Curt, driven by my own wants and needs. Selfish. I've steered clear of commitment my whole life, fucking random women since I was sixteen. So, there's no—" He pressed his fist against his mouth for a few beats, then pushed out his breath. He raised his chin. "There's no way I'm gonna bring a kid into this world knowing the swamp of my gene pool. I come from bad stock, Prim.

End of story."

I stepped closer, grabbing his hand. Feeling it so cold, I rubbed it methodically between my hands. "You're allowed to be angry with him, okay? No child ever deserves to be abandoned and forgotten. But if you can't get past this, this belief you won't be a good father," I said, trying to talk over the pincushion stuck in my throat. "Then I'll get over it. I can do that because you mean everything to me."

He shook his head. "There's no way I'd ever let you sacrifice your dream of being a mother for me."

What about my dream of being yours? Like forever. I took a step backward, bone-level panic threatening. "What exactly are you saying?"

Chase fisted his hands, releasing and tightening them several times. He frowned before cold stone grit cleared his expression. "I love you, Prim, and maybe in my own private way, I always have. Which is why I have to do the right thing. I have to let you go."

"Let me—?"

Go, a small but observant voice filled in. I crossed my arms across my middle, the gears inside my head clicking until the cogs fell into place.

"That's what I walked in on earlier—with you and Thorne." As he bent his head, understanding flowed through me. "So, there's no trip to Texas...no butterflies..."

Chase pinched the bridge of his nose, then shook his head.

I sighed. *Why am I not surprised?* I felt like a hockey puck being batted around by the two of them. I glared at this man I loved and trusted more than anyone, frustration bubbling up inside me. "The least you could have done was talk to me first about this 'never having kids' hangup—and not my *brother*."

I stalked away, practically tripping over Trout as he sprang to his feet. I dropped down on the sofa, and as the dog wedged his body between my legs, I hugged him, rubbing my fingers behind his furry ears.

I gazed into the dog's copper-brown eyes, searching for answers. Chase clearly didn't want a relationship with me, and while his scars from childhood were real, there was no denying they provided him with a convenient exit. Though we'd never talked about children, he obviously knew I wanted a family.

Trout yowled under his breath, burrowing closer to me. *I know, boy. I love him, too.*

It was one thing to fast-track a breakup, but did Chase really think destroying me was the way to do it…?

****

Chase

This was what it felt like to have your heart run through a meat grinder.

"Prim—"

"No," she said, waving me off. "You got to say your bit, now it's my turn." She tossed her hair behind her head, chin lifted. "Let me see if I've got this straight. You love me, but you're letting me go because I'd like to have children one day, and you don't want to rob me of that experience. Which is interesting when you think it's no big deal to rob me of love." Her words dripped with vinegar. "And the reason for all this is you're convinced you come from bad stock, and you'd be a terrible, selfish father."

"It sounds fucked-up when you say it."

"That's because it is fucked-up." She pressed her

fingers to her temples and breathed in and out a few times before lifting her gaze to mine. "You should talk this out with somebody. Like a therapist."

"I'm not really the talker-outer type."

"Oh yeah? And how's that been working for you?"

Fear started to punch the crap out of my long-held reasoning. "Not too bad, actually. Until I fell in love with you."

"And the fact I'd rather be with you *no matter what* makes no difference to you?"

"I can't let you do it, to deny yourself something that's so much a part of who you are. You come from this big, beautiful family. It makes sense you'd want the same thing for yourself. You should have it—you deserve nothing less."

She kissed Trout on the top of his head, pushed up off the sofa, and fumbled with her purse, dropping those damn keys twice before chancing a look at me.

This was it.

She's leaving.

As realization detonated inside my brain, I groped for some way to make her understand. I could stomach a lot of things, but Prim thinking this was somehow her fault wasn't one of them.

"I'm sorry, Prim." Regret scraped the back of my throat. "You've done nothing wrong. It's all me. I'm the one with the fucking problem."

"Maybe. But even if that's true, why did I believe that together we could face anything…?" She shook her head. "And here I thought Avery ruined me." She glared at me, eyes icy blue. "His cheating was a cake walk compared to this mental cluster fuck."

She fisted her hands at her sides, visibly shaking,

and I don't think I'd ever hated myself so much. My screwed-up notions were mine to bear, never meant to be dumped on anyone. Especially Prim.

Inwardly, I cursed my weakness for believing I was worthy of love. I was toxic, selfish, and complete chicken shit.

I'm Curt Bova in every way that matters.

I stepped toward her, and she threw up her hand. "Don't." She circled the room, grabbing easy things— her favorite magazine and the deck of cards we used to play Crazy Eights—and stuffed them in her purse. She walked down the hall to the bathroom, and after hearing a series of drawers raking and banging, I heard her anguished groan.

Minutes later, she reappeared—her hairbrush, bandana, and curling iron sticking out of her bag—and her memory foam pillow shoved under one arm. "I'm off the day after tomorrow. I'll come for the rest of my things then."

"Wait. I can help—"

"Absolutely. Not." Her voice dipped, and she hugged her bag closer to her body. "I don't want your help. *Please*. The least you can do is let me go on *my* terms."

Sure, it was what I should do, only it wasn't what I wanted to do.

I don't fucking want any of this.

I'd spent my life rolling with the current, never feeling the big things, never stumbling over my actions. In my experience, unchecked emotion ended in uncontrollable fallout. That's why I'd stuck to my vow all these years, never allowing myself to think about love, commitment…kids.

As I stared into her tormented gaze, I wished like hell I'd just stayed in my lane and left her alone.

"Prim."

She looked away, over my shoulder, taking measured breaths.

"Please."

She looked at me then, truth quivering on her lips. "Goodbye, Chase."

She pushed past me and out the door, closing it behind her. No slamming, no foot stomping.

Prim very simply.

Very quietly.

Disappeared.

Trout scampered across the room, scratching his paws on the door, whimpering. It took a couple tries before her car engine finally turned over. I listened as the gravel crunched beneath her tires, pain throbbing inside my chest and radiating out to the farthest reaches of my body.

I roared a string of curses to the empty room, then collapsed on the sofa. Trout burrowed under his blanket by the hearth, unwilling to look my way. I rubbed my hands over my eyes, the ache consuming me, cutting off my breath.

I'd known somehow this day would come. That love would crush me like an insect. I loved her, craved her, had wanted to orbit her for the rest of my days. Cold sweat sprang up over my body, and I felt like I'd never feel warm ever again.

Because Primrose Vreeland was my sun.

And like the violent menacing storm cloud I was, I'd swallowed her whole.

Chapter Fourteen

Friday, November 4th 6:20 a.m.
Prim

Dread shadowed me for days. It stalked me. Tailed me. Didn't let up one bit even with exhaustion from pulling a double shift.

Back at the cottage, I laid in my bed at night, restless, staring at the ceiling and talking to myself to keep from losing it. But then I would remember I'd already lost it.

I lost him.

In my more lucid moments, I knew I'd never be free of Chase Bova. His memory was woven into every facet of my being. I would always want the feeling of him pressed against me. Always dream of him, his cognac eyes and sexy grin. Always wonder what might have been if his ghosts hadn't forced him to make such a vow.

Weary of having again reached for and caught something I couldn't keep, I let grief and resentment set up house in my heart.

The last touch, the last laugh.

The last kiss.

When I wasn't using work as a distraction, I collected tidbits from the junkyard of my love life, writing poems and lyrics, plucking out notes on my guitar to match my melancholy heart. It wasn't much consolation, but it was something positive. Or at least that was what I told myself.

After another sleepless night, fatigue pulled at my limbs. I climbed out of bed and shrugged into my robe, padding into the kitchen. As my coffee finished brewing, my phone buzzed in my pocket.

I glanced at the screen and raised it to my ear. "Hey. Tony. You're up early this morning."

I blew over my mug then sipped. I leaned against the counter while Tony ticked off a string of 'he said-she said' lines. I was no stranger to his musician stories. Most of the time, I rather liked his colorful descriptions and embellishments. Then his last sentence whiplashed my brain.

"No effing way."

He continued, and I set the mug on the counter, palm flat on the counter. "Wait. So you're telling me Alisha McCall's interested in one of *my* songs?"

This can't be. Alisha McCall recorded hit songs. Her debut album came out a couple years ago, and it was a huge success. Hands shaking, I pressed the speaker button on my phone, wrapped both hands around the mug, and brought it to my lips.

"I just wanted you to know you'll be getting a call today. You working?" Tony asked.

I confirmed with a groan.

"Don't worry, I've got this. What's a good time, and I'll have them call you then."

I set my coffee cup down so I could hug myself. I wanted to scream and dance and shout all at the same time. I ticked through my schedule at the hospital, gave him my lunch and break times, and took the last swallow of my coffee.

"Prim…? You still with me?"

"Yeah. I'm here. Mildly freaking out, but I'm definitely here." I ran my hand through my hair, turning my face heavenward. "Oh my God, Tony. This is the most exciting news I've ever had. And I need it more than you can imagine." I hesitated, needing his confirmation one more time. "And you're sure? Absolutely sure that Alisha McCall really wants to record 'Yesterday Is All I've Got?' "

He chuckled. "Yes, ma'am. I'm sure. Buckle up, Prim. This is happening. Be sure to call me after you talk to her manager, okay?"

"Absolutely. And thanks, Tony. For everything," I added, swiping my phone closed.

I tapped my foot on the floor, gazing out the kitchen window at the sun rising over my neighbor's house. A breeze ruffled the wind chimes on the porch, and a garbage truck chugged down the street until squeaking brakes signaled its stop.

And a scratchy static crackled through my mind…

Flip a stinking pancake, but I wanted to share this news with Chase. I sighed, fiddling with the tie on my robe, counting the reasons why I shouldn't—*dammit, I wouldn't*—go see him.

I sucked my bottom lip between my teeth. I needed strength and support right now, not the fever dream of Chase Bova.

Slowly, a smile tugged my mouth.

My shoulders lifted as I pictured bluebell eyes and strong soft hands.

Mom. The one person who was always, always, *always* in my corner.

Chapter Fifteen

Friday, November 4th 8:10 a.m.
Chase

Sometimes ideas hit me broadside, like an eighteen-wheeler jackknifing in the road. Hard, fast, and irreversible, the truck committed, crossing the freeway, unable to right itself even as it skids to a halt. Then at other times, ideas weren't as fixed and unrelenting. They percolated inside my head for weeks, months before bubbling up to the surface.

As I played fetch with Trout this morning, I wondered about my internal wiring, why I jackknifed some ideas and percolated others. The one about never fathering children had been a broadside hit, a jackknife decision inspired by my father all those years ago.

If I closed my eyes, I could still see Curt inside the flashy Vegas casino. Since I never got birthday cards from the man, I assumed he had no clue if he'd asked me to meet him on the floor a month ago, I wouldn't have been allowed through the door. Age twenty-one laws meant nothing to a man who spent endless hours chucking coins into slot machines.

I'd arrived early to our meeting on purpose, trolling through rows of tables surrounded with people—all with dollar signs in their eyes. The smoky room, dinging slot machines, and raucous laughter hammered my ears.

Before I finished my first pass through the gallery, I spotted the tall Viking-blond man blowing a kiss over the dice before letting them loose. The crowd hovering around his table hushed, then erupted into cheers. A curvy redhead sprang into his arms, hugging him and kissing his cheek. I stood there, bile churning in my gut, and wondered how a woman as pure and beautiful as my mom had ever turned her heart over to Curt Bova.

Judging by the cigarette bobbing between his grinning lips and the sexy female connected to his hip, things had been going his way at the tables. And when Curt was on a roll, charm oozed out of him like pus from a gangrene wound.

But the night was still young.

I held down a bar stool for a while, until a few losing rounds sidelined Curt's infectious charm, and he sent his squeeze on her way. I was on my third beer when he dropped onto the stool beside me. A man of few words, he got straight to the point of wanting to see me.

Curt wanted a handout. Money. From me and Chase n' Dreams.

I fired off a string of curses with machine gun precision, but he effortlessly deflected it. The standoff was a bitter reminder the man was forged of bulletproof steel, a lump of coal—not a human heart—lodged in his chest.

The night had dragged on, and furious and humiliated, I got my shield tattoo and made a vow. I swore to never father children. There was no way in hell the Bova bloodline would continue through me. I made my pact—with God or Satan, I couldn't be sure—and got the hell out of Vegas.

And that was the last time I'd seen Curt Bova.

I stretched my neck from side to side, shaking off the memory, then glanced at my in-dash GPS.

As I took the exit off I-85 toward Concord, I mulled over my current idea, a percolated one. As asked, I'd left Prim alone to pack up her Elemental with everything important and meaningful in our lives. All the while, I hated myself for being such an emotional mutant. I drank a hell of a lot of liquor, too. But somewhere between the self-loathing and a shot glass, a simple truth had taken shape in my head.

It's like Grandpa's toolshed.

When I was seventeen, Grandpa bet me a hundred bucks I couldn't build him a toolshed. I took the bet, thinking he was getting seriously senile in his old age. When he came home on a Tuesday with a kit that came with directions in six languages and unloaded it in the backyard, I went to work.

"Don't you think it'd be better to study on it first, Chase? Check the weather maybe? You got school, so wouldn't it make sense to wait until the weekend to get started?"

"Are you kidding? I'm not wasting a perfectly good weekend on work."

I checked my side mirrors before switching lanes, laughing at the stupidity that'd spewed out of my cocky teenage mouth.

So, I threw up the toolshed in two and a half afternoons, crooked walls and sagging floor. I remembered standing with my hands on my hips, thinking Grandpa would give me a pass. I mean, the bet was to build a toolshed—no promises about it being a good one.

Yeah, Grandpa was a lot of things, but stupid wasn't

one of them.

After a late night, I made my way home at dawn that Saturday morning. Embarrassment got the best of me, and I cleaned myself up and tore the damn thing apart, plank by plank. I started over again, at the beginning. I took my time, and when Grandpa got home from the mill that evening, the "leaning tower tool shed" had a firm level foundation. I worked the next day and every afternoon for two weeks until I had the job completed. The right way.

And he paid me *two* hundred dollars.

And now I had this slow simmering idea set in my head. I'd screwed up with Prim. *Badly*. And I needed to go back to the beginning, take my time and get to the root of all the mangled feelings I had about Curt Bova.

I didn't know if any of this would matter to Prim in the end. I'd hurt her in ways I was only beginning to understand, and I wasn't sure she'd take me back even if I sorted this out. She was right about one thing though— I needed to talk to someone. But not just anyone. I needed to hash this out with *the* one.

Like the toolshed, I needed to start over.

****

I pulled in at the entrance sign, careful to dodge the potholes in the parking lot. A string of two-story vinyl siding apartments lined the long circular drive, and a small playground sat to the side of the property. I parked between a motorcycle and a hatchback with a pizza delivery sign on top. Skimming my phone for the unit number, I stepped out of my truck and slung on my jacket, Trout close on my heels.

The smell of smoked sausage and onions drifted from a screened window. I muffled a cough, walked to the apartment, and knocked on the door.

And waited.

I exchanged a look with Trout, then knocked again, and this time, I heard footsteps and locks rattling on the other side.

As Curt opened the door, every muscle in my body tensed. I hadn't seen him in a dozen years, but I saw each one reflected in his color and stature. Amidst the vision of thinning hair, hollow cheekbones, and saggy blue jeans, I struggled to find my voice. In height, I towered over him. I shoved my hands in my front pockets. *In my head, I need to tower over him there, too.*

"Curt." I clipped his name, leaning into my reserve of strength and purpose.

"Son. Of a. Bitch." My dad scratched his jaw and cocked his head. "What the hell are you doing here?"

"You alone?" I asked, casting a look over his shoulder.

He nodded, looking down at my feet. "But I see you're not." He bent from the waist, patting Trout and rubbing his hand through his thick coat, then lifted his gaze to mine. "Why don't you two come inside?"

I stepped into his apartment, finding it simple yet clean. Two shelves filled with trophies and ribbons bookended a flat screen television on a stand. A sofa and a recliner with faded seat marks from years of use sat behind a coffee table.

"Want something to drink?" Curt asked, reaching over to silence the TV with the remote.

"You got coffee?"

He snorted. "Yeah, I got coffee."

"Then sure. I like it black."

He nodded. "Have a seat. I'll be back in a few."

As I took off my coat, sat down on the couch, and ran my hands up and down my thighs, my dog made a circle and dropped to my feet. As much to reassure him as me, I reached down to scratch behind his ears and gave him a half smile. Moments later, I heard the pop of an instant cup going into the coffee machine, the whirring sound followed by another pop and beep.

In the years since Vegas, I'd only allowed myself an occasional wondering about Curt. My gaze scanned the room, liquor bottles on a rolling cart and a vape pen on the end table. The only pictures hanging on the wall were of him and a bunch of strangers celebrating at some stock car race. Curt had trained with the best mechanics in the business and once held a top position with a winning pit crew. At sixty years old, he looked spent, lonely, a relic from his checker-flagged past.

Curt stopped in front of me, handed me a mug, and sat down in his recliner. He shifted in the chair and reached for the dial control to turn on the heating pad.

Great. Looks like arthritic joints run in the Bova family, too.

I took a sip of coffee and cleared my throat. "Guess you're wondering why I'm here."

He steepled his fingers under his chin. "I'm not much for wondering. I'd rather just wait until the deal is on the table."

I nodded, and a string of long seconds ticked by. Trout raised his head, shook it, then lowered it on his front paws.

Curt turned, flicking his head in my direction. "Nice ink you got there. You had it long?"

My gaze fell to my bicep then lifted to his face. "About twelve years."

"A shield, huh?" He paused, bringing his vape pen to his mouth. He inhaled then exhaled. "What's a smart good-looking guy like you need protection from? I know you're not anything like me, loan sharks hot on your tail."

"It's more of a *who* than a *what*." Our gazes locked, and after a couple beats, awareness flickered in his brown eyes. My courage mounted. "I got it in Vegas, that time I met you there. After you hit me up for money in the casino."

Curt blew out a breath, and his chest fluttered under his thin T-shirt. "Not one of my better moments."

I slurped my coffee before setting the mug on the table. I cupped my hands over my knees. "After I left you, I found a tattoo studio."

"Were you drunk?" he asked over a chuckle.

"Hell, no." Schooling my emotions, I slowly turned toward him. "I was fucking angry. Humiliated that my own damn father only saw me as a meal ticket. I needed to get you out of my life."

"So, you tattooed a symbol of protection on your arm. From me. I get it."

"But that's not all. I needed you out of my body, too." I fisted my hands together between my knees. "After the shit you pulled on me, I vowed to never have children, never pass on to another human being the sorry-ass genes I got from you. It's been more than a decade, and I've stayed true to my vow."

I lowered my head and stared at my feet, silently warring with the youngster I was then and the man I was today. What had been so logical at the time, had been my North Star guide in the years since, now seemed unraveled and unhinged. Trout inched closer to me, settling his head on my tennis shoe, which in dog language meant *I've got you.*

"My guess is it's not going so good for you now. Otherwise you wouldn't be here on my doorstep."

I shook my head.

"You wanna to talk about it?"

"I thought I did. I'm not so sure now."

He pulled on his vape pipe. "Sounds to me like you've put a lot of energy into hating me. Like I'm an altar or something. Only now maybe your happiness has become the sacrificial lamb."

"Jesus. I never pegged you as the spiritual type," I said, deadpan.

He chuckled under his breath. "Nah, just an old man who's live too hard and too long. I own my mistakes— all of them. And I'll take them to my grave."

I absorbed his words, searching for clarity in his self-deprecating statement. Grandpa taught me all a man can do is make the best choices he can with what he knows and who he is at the time. No one has the benefit of hindsight when there was nothing but the future staring him in the face.

That was how Grandpa explained why Curt left his daughter and grandchildren—the man simply wasn't made of the right stuff.

That was why he told Carrie and me to forgive him, like he and Mom had.

That was also why the no-kids vow made sense to me. Or it had, until Prim came into my life.

I dragged my hands through my hair and slumped on the sofa. "It's just—well, this vow made sense to me. I was too much like you. I wanted to live life on my terms, go where I wanted when I wanted. I've traveled across North America—making a good living doing something I love—and never once had a girlfriend. Never once had any regrets."

Curt chewed on the inside of his cheek. "Until now."

I nodded.

"Damn, Chase. Are you forgetting half of you—hell, *most* of you—comes from your mother? Holly had more love in her baby toe than I had in my entire body. I knew it. She knew it. Everybody knew it." His voice crackled, and he coughed into his fist. When he recovered, he continued. "So if you think you're doing mankind a favor by not bringing another Curt into the world, well fine. But I think you're forgetting something. You're also robbing it of the chance to know another Holly." He swallowed, blinking away from my face. "It's a damn shame God always takes the best ones first, Chase. And your mother…she was the finest woman I ever knew."

I flexed my hands by my sides. "I'm not going to talk to you about Mom."

"Then spit it out. What do you want from me?"

"I think," I began, my words scratchy like sandpaper. "I think…I want to forgive you."

He shook his head briskly. "No. No, I don't deserve forgiveness."

"Yeah, you don't. But I need it. So I can move on with my life."

Curt drew on his vape pipe, smoke curling from the corners of his mouth, then dropped it in his lap.

"All right. Do whatever the hell you need to do." He gripped the arms on his recliner, then cocked his head at me. "You know, you may favor me in looks, but the likeness ends there. You got your mother's good heart and your grandpa's good sense." He took a breath and released it slowly. "And since we're airing out all our shit, I want to tell you one thing. I never should've asked you to meet me in Vegas. It was wrong of me to try to drag you into my problems. I never intended to mess with your head. I just needed some money."

In the lull that followed his admission, I finished my coffee. Curt unmuted the TV giving a little white noise to the quiet in the room. Trout lifted his head with the referee's whistle on the football game and shifted to a sitting position.

I glared at Curt. I was ready to rally, and he was damn well going to look me in the eyes when I did.

When our gazes met, I slapped my hands on my knees. "How could I have known anything about your intentions, huh? All I got was the greed in your voice, the gleam in your eye when you thought I'd be your meal ticket. I'm not the same person today as I was all those years ago. I was young and cocky. And this idea to get you out of my system hit me broadside—like right while I was getting this tattoo inked on my arm." I glanced down and rubbed my hand over it before meeting his gaze again. "Vowing to never father children meant not passing along my bad genes. Which helped me get past you and all the shit from my past. But now, this vow is keeping me from being with the woman I love."

"I want it all, Curt. I'm a selfish bastard, and I want a life with her. And kids. It's what I want and need more than anything in the world."

With that realization, I pushed past the decades of resentment, through the emotional wreckage of my youth and shot up to my feet.

"I forgive you, Curt. For everything. God help me, I

Seconds ticked by like minutes, and I thought I must be having a heart attack, every breath a constricting slice beneath my sternum. In time, I slowly pulled back and met her gaze. "Please tell me what happened."

I listened while Mrs. Vreeland relayed information from the first responders. Apparently Prim's Elemental stalled on the highway. The road was slick from a rain shower, and an approaching SUV clipped her rear end, sending her car into a tailspin and down a ravine.

My body shook with fear. I didn't need a medical degree to know blunt force trauma, flipping over in a vehicle, was bad.

Somehow I got to my feet and dropped into the chair beside Mrs. Vreeland. As she held my hand, I realized there were people scattered across the room, all waiting for news about Prim.

Billie and her husband, Mark. Chloe sitting in her dad's lap, clutching her teddy bear in her arms.

Officer Brent Conard, who I learned had been one of the first to arrive to the crash.

The EMT Brandon, and a couple of the nurses I'd met when I came by with coffee and pastries on Prim's early shifts.

"Just pray, son. Pray hard. Prim's strong, and she's a fighter. She's not alone in there. God is with her."

I nodded, and easing back in my chair, I closed my eyes.

And for the longest time, I prayed.

****

Time in a hospital waiting room moved on its own continuum. Seconds passed like minutes, minutes like hours, distorted with uncertainty and unknowing.

I sat, I paced, and when I stepped outside to escape

179

the antiseptic hospital smell, even the fresh air fell flat in my lungs. Thoughts of never again standing outdoors with Prim, sunshine kissing her cheeks, pummeled my brain.

When I went inside again, I shifted gears back to praying, imagining what life would look like after we left this room. I was done marking time. I wanted to cherish it—every single moment of it—with Prim.

Please, God. Don't take her away from me. Please don't give me another reason to hate Novembers.

Just before four o'clock, a surgeon in scrubs entered the waiting room. Ace and his mother converged on her, and I stepped in close behind them.

"She made it through surgery without additional complications. Her condition is critical but stable."

Billie stepped in beside me and grabbed my hand. The doctor went on to describe the injuries—internal bleeding near a lung, a concussion, and numerous external lacerations. She tempered that with some good news—no spine or nerve damage, no bleeding on the brain, and strong vitals.

"She'll be in the ICU for at least the next twelve to fourteen hours. I'm sorry, but I can only allow two of you in the room."

I watched Ace and his mom exchange looks, then Ace put her hand in mine.

"I think Mom and Chase need to be there," Ace said on a heavy breath, stepping aside.

****

For the first six hours of Prim's stay in the ICU, Mrs. Vreeland and I sat by her bedside. Around ten o'clock, the nurse led her to a room where she could get some sleep.

For the next eight hours, Ace took his mom's place, and we watched in silence as the machines hooked up to her periodically clicked and bleeped.

At dawn, the surgeon came in to tell us they were moving Prim to a private room.

"She's had no fever and shows no signs of additional internal complications. Her vitals are getting stronger, but she's going to need sleep. We'll keep her comfortable and quiet in her own room. And don't worry, I'll keep a very close eye on her."

After thanking the doctor, Ace and I engulfed each other in a hug, then he left to tell the others the news.

I gazed down at Prim, and when I swallowed, I tasted tears in my throat. She looked so small and fragile, but Thorne was right. Inside she was as tough as a little bulldozer.

A thousand times tougher than me.

Suddenly, all the fear and tension caged inside my body fled, and I stumbled backward, sliding down the wall to the floor. I landed with a thud, and I stretched my legs out in front of me. Leaning my head against the wall, I pulled air into my lungs and let the tears stinging my eyes run down my cheeks. I thanked God repeatedly for taking care of Prim.

When I could, I wiped my eyes with the back of my hand, climbed to my feet, and walked to her bedside.

I brushed my fingers against hers. "You've come this far, babe. I'm here with you. With you forever."

Chapter Seventeen

Sunday, November 6th 9:20 a.m.
Prim

"She's awake."
I blinked at the sound of the words.
"Mom, Chase. She's awake."
I recognized Goldie's voice.
I knew who Mom was.
But Chase…?
In time, a nurse stepped into my line of vision, politely asking if family would mind waiting outside for a few minutes. She checked my vitals and monitored the bags attached to my IV. I didn't know her well, but I'd seen her around the hospital on occasion. She stepped over to her laptop, tapping on the keyboard. I found her voice pleasant, but what she said made my head swim.

"And the ICU nurse said your boyfriend never left your side yesterday. He's been with you here, too. The whole time." She looked at me with a smile of sympathetic envy, and my stomach turned over. "It's so sweet how protective and devoted he is."

As her words sank in, so did reality. Chase wasn't my boyfriend. He was just another disappointment. A selfish disappointment who cared more about a vendetta against his father than me.

Need suddenly filled my heart. "When you're done,

would you ask my mom to come in?" At her questioning brow, I added, "Just her. Please."

The nurse gave me a "poor thing" look, and I instantly hoped I'd never given that to any of my patients. I clutched the bedsheet in my hands, conceding now wasn't the time to evaluate my bedside manner, and waited for her to leave.

Moments later, my mom came in and pulled the rolling chair to my bed.

"Hey, sweet girl." She kissed my hand, tears pulling on her eyelashes. "I've never been so happy to see you."

"Oh, Mom." My voice tightened and my eyes heated, and everything felt so fresh, raw. "I don't really remember what happened—just stalling out and then spinning." I shook my head but stopped because it hurt. It felt heavy, like five times too big. I lifted my hand to the dressing wrapped around my forehead.

"You suffered a concussion. And some internal bleeding." I looked down at my arms, and she continued. "Some cuts and bruises. But you're alive, Prim. And we're going to take good care of you. When you're released, you're coming home with me. I'm still a pretty good mom-nurse."

"You're the best mom-nurse." Our gazes met, and emotion threatened to spill out of me again. "Thank you for taking care of me. You always do. I love you."

She gently touched my arm. "You've had so many people here loving you and praying for you. Well, the whole family, of course."

"Wait. Even Thorne and Sage?"

"They got here last night."

I stared at the white tile ceilings. "But they're so busy. I hate they had to drop everything for me." I sighed. "For this."

"You couldn't have kept them away. Your brothers and sisters love you so much. I love you, too. And so does someone else."

I knew patients often felt confused after trauma. After basic human survival and adrenaline subsided, the brain needed time to reset, recalibrate. Rationally, I knew this. But right now I was light years away from rational. "I don't understand why Chase is here. And I definitely don't want to talk about him."

"Fair enough. I don't want you thinking about any of this right now. Just rest and eat a little something. Listen to the doctor and do exactly what she says so we can take you home."

I gave her a gentle nod. "I think I'll close my eyes for a while." I formed my next sentence carefully in case the "selfish disappointment" was still outside my room. "Will you tell my sisters and brothers I'll see them in a little while? And that I love them?"

Mom nodded, kissed my cheek, and quietly left the room.

Chapter Eighteen

About Two Weeks Later
Monday, November 21st 9:15 a.m.
Chase

When I was fourteen, my grandpa sat me down for a talk. *Not the sex one.* He did that when I was twelve, after catching me in the bathroom with a porn magazine. No, this talk was for a confused teenage kid who couldn't make sense out of girls.

What Grandpa went on to explain was women were shifty like the winds. Some days they blew right along with you. Other days, their gusts smacked you square in the face. He said for me to be patient, and between today and someday, the right woman would come along, and I'd weather all her winds because I loved her.

Grandpa was a wise man.

As I stepped out of my truck, I left the windows down and tossed Trout a bone. The crunch of pea-sized gravel beneath my boots mixed with my thoughts. I'd been an ass to take a beautiful person like Prim and throw her wind patterns off kilter. She was no longer a sultry sea breeze. She was a wary mountain gust. And damn if I didn't deserve every bit of her turbulence.

Prim had been home from the hospital for almost a week, and since she still hadn't asked to see me, I went by the farm every day to see Ace for an update.

I found his door open, the big man reclined in his chair, glasses low on the bridge of his nose, a green bar ledger sheet in his hands. The Three Creeks farm office smelled of pine, hay, and tobacco, scents infused in the room that'd been around for a hundred years. Technology had changed farming, but legacy and grit still thrived in the Vreeland family and their centuries-old enterprise.

As a kid, it was hard for me to stand here in the presence of Gray Vreeland and not feel small. Today, knowing what I needed to share with his eldest son, I somehow felt the same damn way.

I knocked on the door, and Ace straightened in his chair, tossing the sheet over a half-eaten donut. He motioned to the chair in front of his desk. "Been expecting you."

I took the seat but not before spotting a small tick in his jaw. "What? Is something wrong?" I gripped the edge of his desk. "Is Prim—"

"No, she's fine." I fell back in the chair and gulped a breath. "It's just you've been coming here every day like a stray cat hungry for scraps."

"What can I say? You keep feeding me, so I keep coming back." I rubbed my hand over my neck. "And just in case I haven't said it enough, I appreciate it."

Ace nodded and shifted in his chair. "Well, I can tell you Prim looks more like herself today. Yesterday, the doctor removed the bandages, and her cuts are mostly healed." He scratched his head. "She told her she's doing better, better than expected. She's just gotta keep resting and building her strength before she can return to work…or think about moving back to her place."

"What *place*?" The word snagged in my throat.

"Oh, I guess you wouldn't know about this." He grumbled under his breath before continuing. "Before the accident, she rented the cottage again. After she moved out of your house."

That stung. She'd gone to her old place just days after leaving me. Which meant she wanted her independence. "But surely she's not ready to leave Three Creeks. She should stay here as long as possible. It's good for her to be looked after."

He scratched his head. "Is that all you've got?"

"Dammit, Ace. What else do you want me to say?"

"You wouldn't leave her bedside in the hospital. Now, you don't go anywhere near her."

"I'm trying to respect Prim's wishes. In case you haven't heard, she wants nothing to do with me. That was true before the accident. It's true now."

"Oh, for the love of"—Ace plowed his hands through his hair—"I can't believe I'm standing here telling *you* how to make it right with my sister. This isn't brain surgery, Chase. It's love. And if it's real, then it's *real* damn simple."

"Am I supposed to camp outside her door or—"

"You did at the hospital."

I cupped my hands around my mouth, then blew out my breath. I met his gaze. "Which was before I learned she didn't want to see me again."

"Don't shit me. You knew she loved you, and you knew how she felt about having a family before the accident. Why would things have changed?"

"I don't know." *Maybe because my vow no longer means anything to me.*

"Look, if you've got something on your mind, something you need to say, then say it. Put it out there and let Prim decide. At least you'd know you did all you could—"

Need was a hungry animal. Telling Prim about Curt and all the crap I'd locked away for so many years had need clawing at my gut. But I wasn't sure I could give it an ass-kicking just yet.

"—and then maybe both of you could move on."

"Move on?" I croaked, broadcasting my emotion. "Move *on*? That's the last thing I want."

Ace walked away from his desk, shaking his head. "It's what you told my sister, right? You let her go."

"I had my reasons but—"

"Yeah. Whatever."

Undeterred, I pulled a small velvet box from my pocket and placed it in Ace's hand. He lifted the lid and blew out his cheeks.

"Holy shit. If this isn't déjà vu."

I shook my head. "Come again…?"

"It's just Max Corda stood right here in my office a couple years ago—with all his regrets and shit—and asked for my blessing to marry Goldie."

"And you obviously said yes."

"I did."

I sighed around a faint smile. "So there's hope."

"Or a very disturbing pattern in the men who love my sisters. Jesus, who knew Mark would be the only one to fall in love the old-fashioned way."

"Yeah, I've never done simple."

"You've never done monogamy either."

The truth of his words bit, but I pushed back. "I'm in love with your sister. She changed my life."

"Have you forgotten children come with the Primrose package?"

I shook my head. "I can't go into details, but just know I've worked it out in my head. I don't feel that way anymore. I just need the chance to tell Prim—ask her to marry me." I swallowed hard. "If you'll give me your blessing."

He cocked his head. "And if I don't...?"

"I'll ask your mom."

"Think she's in your corner, huh?"

I stared at my feet before fixing my gaze on Ace. "There are three women who've shaped my life. First is my mom. She loves me unconditionally—in life and in death. Then there's Carrie. She gives me the kick-butt love I need." Ace chuckled. "Then there's your mom. From the time I met Thorne in kindergarten, she treated me like another son. So did your dad, God bless him."

I steadied my voice. "I don't deserve your mom's kindness, but I'm grateful for it. So if you withhold your blessing, I'll have no choice but to beg for hers. Nothing's going to stop me from going after the woman I love. I can make Prim happy, take care of her. I want everything with her—a life together *and* kids." I rubbed my knuckles over my mouth. "If she'll have me."

Ace closed the small box and handed it to me. "I don't know what's caused you to do a complete one-eighty, but I believe you. You're a good guy. You've got my blessing, and I wish you luck, man. Prim's loving and forgiving, but you've got to earn her trust again."

I tucked the box inside my pocket. "I've got a lot of groveling ahead of me."

"True." Ace scratched his jaw. "But you need to come clean with her. Help her understand what's underneath all that personality and charm—to know what makes you tick."

I nodded, my gaze flickering to a family photograph on Ace's desk. I reached for it, studying the picture and all it represented.

Loyalty. Family. Roots.

"Nothing means more to me than my family, Chase. Maybe one day, I'll be able to call you my brother."

"I'd like that."

"But if Prim says no, I need your word you'll respect it. I won't have you interfering in her life and causing trouble."

"I've steered clear of her, giving her time to heal and think, haven't I?"

"Because right now you have hope." He tipped his chin at my pocket. "Inside your heart and tucked away in that velvet box. If she turns you away, hope goes down the toilet."

I groaned, knowing only an idiot would ignore the logic and warning in his words. Prim held the cards, wielded the power. If I'd done too much damage to win back her trust, then I'd have no other choice but to clean up the wreckage and go on my way.

"Well, I guess I'm gonna find out what lies between today and someday." As a crease formed on his brow, I shook out my shoulders. "Means I'm gonna hang on to hope for now. But you can trust me. I'll know when to walk away."

Ace shook my hand, then I walked out the door. Outside, I felt like the underdog fighter stepping into the ring. Only my opponent wasn't an opponent at all. She was a five foot seven, fit little swimming machine, with bluebell eyes that sparkled when we kissed. She was creative, artistic, and a lifesaving nurse.

She's my heart.

Chapter Nineteen

Monday, November 21st 10:04 a.m.
Prim

I'd always erred on the side of caution whenever a woman's head needed shaving due to an injury. Sometimes trimming a small section gave the doctors all the access they needed, saving the patient emotional grief. Some might call it vanity, but most women considered their hair a part of their identity, right up there with skin tone and eye color.

As I gazed in my bedroom mirror at the laceration at my temple—now with stitches removed—I gave thanks to my colleagues for offering me the same consideration. *Tiffany really looks out for me.* A smile ghosted my lips, grateful no stubbly blonde hair spiked up from my hairline. I pulled my sweater down over my head, finger combed some longer hair over the neatly trimmed spot at my ear, then made my way downstairs.

I grabbed a blueberry bran muffin from a tray on the counter and poured a glass of orange juice. I wiggled onto a stool at the island bar and flipped through my newsfeed while I ate.

Then my emails.

Then texts.

Lastly, I opened my calendar.

Thanksgiving is three days away...

But I wasn't sure I could do it this year.

It was as if Vista Falls had turned into an alternate dimension since my breakup with Chase—and that was before adding the injuries from the crash into the mix.

But honestly, I couldn't blame the accident for the cactus-patch feelings in my heart. They'd been pricking and poking me since Chase's big Halloween unmasking. In a grand charade, he'd pulled me in only to push me away. At least in choosing no kids over his relationship with me, he'd gotten something. His freedom and staying true to his vow.

But me? I came up empty.

Again.

I spotted Mom's "last minute" grocery list on the counter and grabbed the pen beside it. Cranberries, oranges, self-rising flour, pecans...*sweet potatoes*. I clicked the pen with my thumb, drawing swirls and hearts around the edges of the paper, the memory of Chase joking about my sweet potato casserole moving through my mind. He'd come with supper and parts to fix my kitchen sink that night. He liked taking care of me. He liked being my rescuer.

As a shiver climbed up my spine, I let those moments of early flirtation fade into nothingness. I'd learned the hard way I wasn't enough for him. Though Chase had touched my heart and restored my sexual confidence, our relationship was dysregulated, triggering. Like fingernails-scraping-down-a-chalkboard unsettling.

I groaned. *I can get through this*. Maybe I could offer to take the Thanksgiving day shift, give another nurse the chance to spend time with family.

But Thorne would strangle me. Then Goldie would

kill me. I knew my five siblings would never leave me alone. They'd shower me with hugs and kisses and push my beautiful niece and nephews into my arms to help heal my broken heart.

I have to get through this. It was one day, and then I could focus on settling back into my cottage, my job, my songwriting…and Alisha McCall's recording of "Yesterday Is All I've Got."

While that last thought made me smile, another buzzed about in my head.

The distance between today and someday still felt daunting.

I had thought someday I'd try being a traveling nurse. *Nope.*

Or someday I'd find a good man to love and who'd love me back. *Not yet.*

Or perhaps someday I'd own a home. *Not likely.*

But at least one thing had gone right. I crossed my arms on the countertop and let my smile slowly grow. Alisha recording my song was the single clear note in my life of minor chords. *This someday is happening.*

I finished my breakfast and put the dishes in the dishwasher. Tractors hummed in the distance, and an engine cut off just outside the kitchen window. As I tucked my phone in the pocket of my jeans, the sound of barking and scratching from behind the kitchen door lifted in the air.

I opened the door, and Trout ran right through my legs, circling me before rubbing his head against my thigh. I put a hand between his ears and tousled his fur. An unexpected joy bubbled up inside me knowing if Trout was here, Chase couldn't be far behind.

"I'm glad to see you, too," I said to the dog looking

at me with cinnamon sugar eyes. He tossed his gaze to Chase, and my stomach fell straight through the floor.

"Hello, Prim."

As my name crossed his lips, I had to toss out an anchor to keep my heart from drifting away…and over to him. In those two words, I imagined a mixture of others not spoken. *I've missed you. I need you more than air. I want you and our life together. And nothing else.*

I tamped down the ridiculous thoughts before they became a song in my head, truly hating how *he* was the only song in my head.

And probably always would be.

"He's missed you." Chase dropped his chin to his chest, then lifted it, meeting my gaze. "We both have."

I gave his dog one last pat on the back, then straightened, hands on my hips. Inside, I strapped on my armor, ready to play the soldier for my heart.

"I've missed Trout, too." I watched Chase flinch, his shoulders dipping with my omission of his name, and I steeled my voice. "Bringing him along with you isn't playing fair."

He shoved his hands in the pockets of his jeans. "I'm a desperate man. I need every advantage I can get."

I shook my head, laughing humorlessly. "Whatever. Why don't you tell me what you're doing here?"

Chase whistled for his dog, motioning for him to sit by the door, then turned to me. "I heard about 'Yesterday Is All I've Got.' Everyone's talking about it." A smile stretched his mouth. "I'm so proud of you. I knew your music was amazing, and now the rest of the world will know, too."

I managed a quiet, "Thank you."

As he tried to close the distance between us, instinct

kicked in, and I stepped backward.

"Are you afraid of me?" His tone sounded rough, stunned.

I bit my bottom lip. "No. But I'm afraid of how I feel when I'm around you. This isn't good for me. So again, why are you here…?"

His chest fell, as though my words had punched the air out of his lungs. He regarded me for a few long moments then said, "For you. I'm here for you. I love you, Prim. I'm so sorry I put you through all this, but I'm here. Asking for another chance."

His little speech bashed my heart. He'd told me before he loved me, and I blindly believed him. I clearly had weights in my shoes because my feet wouldn't do what my brain was demanding. *Show him to the door.*

But I found my words. "No."

The unflappable Chase Bova swayed just a little bit.

I took a deep breath. "You heard me. No. You don't get to do this to me again."

He tried to reach for me. "I hurt you. I know that. But things have changed—I've changed. Please, just let me prove it to you."

"I don't trust you anymore," I said, my stomach twisting into a knot. "We're toxic. Our values don't line up. It was more important for you to disguise your feelings behind a pathetic vow and say, 'Oh, I've got to let you go—' "

"Christ, I know what I said."

"—than to man up and work things out together."

"But I'm here now. I've worked it out, and I'm good with it. All of it."

"Why, Chase? Why now…?"

"Because I love you, and I want to marry you." He

grabbed a box from his jacket pocket and opened it, turning it to me.

Flip a pancake…

My knees trembled, but I managed to take in a clean breath. I'd always imagined I would have a lot of feelings teeming through my body when the man I loved asked me to marry him.

But that wasn't what was happening, right here, right now. No joyous influx of emotions.

Just one feeling flooded my heart. *Distrust.*

I straightened my back and stilled my knees. While the doctor had patched me up, I'd done a little sewing of my own…to my heart. The seams weren't industrial strength, but they were set and secure. And I wasn't about to let Chase rip them apart.

But I did want answers, closure.

I narrowed my gaze. "And what is this big *'it'* you've suddenly figured out?"

"Look, I love you. I've never felt this way about anyone, and I don't want to lose you. We're great together. And I love kids." He stepped forward as if to prevent my protest. "I'll love *our* kids. I'm going all in with you, Prim—in *us*. Can't you please just accept I'm better now, and let's do this thing?"

While he'd strung together a lot of charming words, it wasn't an explanation. It was a persuasive argument, fashioned like the bait he dangled on the end of his fishing line. Only I wasn't biting anymore.

I gazed into his eyes, brown irises flecked with a gold relaying the war waging behind them. *Just tell me the truth.*

Trust me with your past.

And then he blinked and looked away, and I knew

which Chase had won the battle.

He snapped the box lid closed and dropped it in his pocket. "I guess I was wrong. I thought you loved me."

"I do love you. That's not the issue here. I need to understand who Chase Bova really is, because what you're giving me right now is a bunch of crap. And until you're ready to let your guard down, will you please just *stop*?"

He flinched. "If I leave you alone, you'll think I don't care. If I stay—"

"Staying isn't an option. I'm not okay when I'm this close to you. You're way too much for me."

"If you need time, I'll wait. I'd do anything to make things right between us."

"You know what I need, Chase." Even as I said the words, a knife scraped through my heart. "I need *you*. All of you."

His voice dropped an octave. "I'm not sure I can do that."

Bitterness swept through me. While Chase and I shared a connection, our bond had cracked at the first sign of challenge. He'd placed his heart under restricted access years ago, and no one—least of all me—stood a chance at breaking the code.

As he leaned forward and kissed my forehead, tears clouded my vision. He traced my cheek with his thumb, then rubbed it across my lower lip. The gesture stirred me, and the temptation to forget how we got to this point hung between us.

"Goodbye, Prim."

Chase whistled for Trout, then walked out the door. I listened for his footsteps on the porch steps. I took an enormous breath, imagining what might have been if I'd only let him stay.

I crawled onto the sofa, curled into a ball, and wept.

Chapter Twenty

Tuesday, December 6th 4:10 p.m.
Chase

I spent the next couple weeks in a committed relationship with my favorite scotch at a barroom on the outskirts of town. I saved little time for home because Prim's ghost lived there, in every wall, counter, and surface.

I fed my dog, but I ignored strategic planning meetings with the Chase n' Dreams team. I didn't go swimming, and I didn't fish either. I ate nothing unless it came straight off the shelf or could be nuked in the microwave. I bathed and took out the trash when I remembered to—which judging by the goat stink lifting from my skin and permeating my house, wasn't nearly enough.

I'd never been a mental case, but then my life had never been such a shitshow. Even at what I'd always considered my lowest point—my disastrous showdown with Curt in Las Vegas—I'd never sunk to the level of pond scum. Even Trout found a stray cat lurking at the edge of the woods better company than me.

I opened the front door and stepping onto the porch, noticed rain falling in a steady drizzle. I moved forward, nearly tripping over a box. I read the note attached.

Call me when you get this. And eat the food. All of

it. If I don't hear from you in twenty-four hours, I'm coming for you. Carrie.

I stretched my arms above my head, turning my head left and right, and my neck popped like a pickaxe cracking through ice. I swore under my breath and scratched my stomach, and as a white SUV turned into my driveway, I ducked inside for a shirt. When I stepped back outside, Carrie stood on the porch, holding Charlotte's hand.

Carrie glared at the unopened box. "You didn't think I'd come, did you?"

Ignoring my sister, I bent down to Charlotte. "Hey, Kitten. Don't you look cute in your little Santa Claus sweatshirt."

Charlotte sniffed the air. "When I smell like you, Mommy makes me take a bath."

I smiled and stood straight. "Well, you're really lucky to have a mommy who looks after you. I'm just a crusty old fisherman left to take care of myself." As Carrie bent to pick up the box, I threw out my hands. "Hey, I can get that."

"Yeah, 'cause you're so good at taking care of things." She rolled her eyes then walked inside.

Charlotte and I followed suit, only my niece plopped down on the sofa and flipped the channels to the nearest cartoon, and I marched on to the gallows. I heard the tap of cans on the kitchen counter, the crinkle of plastic bags. I fell into a chair and finished buttoning my shirt.

When she had the last of the items tucked away in the pantry, she turned on me. "You look like absolute shit."

"Apparently, I smell like it, too."

"And since when do you not check your texts?"

"I check them. But I only reply to people I actually want to talk to."

She crossed her arms over her chest. "You have no idea how badly I was hoping I'd find you passed out on the sofa today. I really wanted to dump a big bucket of cold water over your sorry head."

"That would've only pissed me off."

"At least it would've been a reaction—something to indicate you're not just a worthless blob—" She struggled for her words and landed on "—of *worthlessness.*"

I laughed, and when she started to swat me with the kitchen towel, she scrunched her nose at its dingy toilet water color.

She slung it into the sink. "For the love of God, I'm getting a cleaning service over here first thing in the morning."

I folded my arms on the table, lowered my forehead to my hands, and spoke to the tabletop. "Don't, Carrie. I'm not in the mood for this shit. Thank you for coming over here and bringing me food." I lifted my head before continuing. "But I've got this. I know what I'm doing."

"You don't know shit." She dragged a chair over beside mine and ran her fingers through my hair. She touched my cheek. "I'm worried about you. You're not okay." Her gaze swung around the kitchen. "*This* is not okay." When I groaned, she added, "Talk to me, Chase. I'm not leaving until you do."

Thankfully, Charlotte called out for a snack, and Carrie left to check on her. When she returned, the same fire still burned in her tone. "Now out with it. The whole town knows you and Prim split. There has to be a way to fix things."

"I wish there was, but it's over. She called it. She wants nothing to do with me."

"She's a beautiful intelligent woman who until recently was living here with you and crazy in love. So were you. Now tell me. *What happened*?"

I blew out my breath, pressed my fist to my forehead, then started at beginning. I walked her through every sad step, taking caution at one particular turn.

"I went to see Curt." The silence grew tight between us. "He—or rather the wall I'd built around myself for protection from him—was ruining me."

Carrie clasped her hands together in a fist and listened while I emptied my guts about Vegas, my tattoo, and my vow.

"But why on earth didn't you ever say anything to me? You shouldn't have had to go through this alone all these years."

I shrugged. "I didn't consider it a problem that needed solving. I made my pact, and it suited me just fine."

She rubbed her finger over her lip. "No wonder you've never been serious with anyone."

"Yep. That was the plan."

"But you said you went to see Dad?"

"I went to see *Curt*." I cleared my throat. "When Prim and I split, she said I needed to talk to someone. And she was right."

"And that someone was Curt?"

I nodded.

"And did you get what you needed?"

I thought about her question and the confusion it would've triggered just weeks ago. Dark feelings had littered my life, my heart, for so many years. Though the burden was only recently lifted, I couldn't help but feel hopeful.

I released a pent up breath and held her gaze. "I forgave him, Carrie. I did what you, Mom, and Grandpa did all those years ago. And it was like instantly, I felt all the anger and resentment leave my body. For most of my life, I thought my heart was too small for love in the long haul. But I was wrong, it was never too small. It was just in lockdown."

"And have you told Prim this?"

"I told her I loved her, and I wanted to marry her and have a family. I even showed her the engagement ring I bought." I shook my head. "And nothing. She said she didn't trust me anymore."

Carrie touched my arm, squeezing it gently. "No, I meant have you shared this story with her? Have you been honest about your feelings, about all the things you've kept locked up inside?"

"I can't. I don't know how to talk to someone like that. What do I do? Just hand her the knife and let her fillet me like a fish?"

"If you really love her, there's no way you *can't* tell her."

A tug of war raged between my head and my heart. Back in high school, I'd known Prim was too good for me, and I'd never so much as sniffed in her direction. And all these years later, I still knew she was out of my league. I was trying to catch a perfect largemouth bass with a scrawny worm.

But I went after her anyway because I wanted her.

Needed her.

I love her.

I scrubbed my hands down my face, groaning from

somewhere deep in my soul. "I really hate love, you know that?"

Carrie nodded, the corners of her mouth turning upward.

"I hate the whole ass-knocking, heart-hugging, breath-stealing thing."

"I get it, Chase. I do. But if you really love her…"

I diverted my gaze, took a deep breath and plunged ahead. "You're right. I love her so much. I know what I need to do."

Carrie jumped up, leaned over, and planted a kiss on my cheek. As she ruffled my hair, stirring up the essence of goat stink, she wrinkled her nose and mustered a smile. "Hey, why don't you go take a *really* long hot shower while I make you and Charlotte some supper?"

I gazed at my sister. Carrie looked so much like our mother, and at times like these, she acted like her, too. She'd always made a place in her life for me, even when I'd go weeks sometimes without even calling her. Guilt seeped into my bones.

"You know, this change in me isn't just about Prim. It's about me being a good person, a better man. I haven't always been the best brother, and I'm sorry. I'm going to make it up to you. I promise."

"I don't want the *best* brother," she said, letting her grin grow. "But I'd love to have the best version of Chase Bova, please. New and improved?"

"Eh, probably more like reconditioned."

She laughed, and I laughed, and suddenly Charlotte's giggles drifted in from the den.

"Thanks for being here for me, Carrie. I really love you. So damn much." When I went in for a hug, she playfully waved her hand at me and pinched her nose. I grinned. "Right. Shower."

As I made my way into the bathroom, I thought about how I'd fought for most things in my life. I fought hard and in time, usually won. Being bullheaded had served me well, only I wasn't sure I could win over Prim this time. She was loving and kind, but also pretty damn stubborn.

I turned on the water, dragged my shirt over my head, and yanked off my jeans, tossing the smelly clothes into a pile. I stepped into the shower and turned the temperature higher, letting the heat penetrate my muscles. I had to wonder if I had enough fight left in me to change Prim's mind. As much as I wanted a future with her, there was a real possibility I'd done too much damage for her to forgive me.

But to give up, to walk out of Prim's life, was impossible. I had to find the words, tell her my story, and accept whatever came next. Capturing Prim's heart was like trying to lasso the wind, and I was going to do what Grandpa said and weather all her winds because I loved her.

Chapter Twenty-One

Tuesday, December 6th 4:10 p.m.
Prim

"One fifty-five over ninety-seven, Mr. Langston." The tear of hook and loop adhesive ripped through the air as I removed the blood pressure cuff from my patient. "It's good you came in today."

"Yeah, I didn't want to get out in the rain, but my wife didn't give me much choice." His gaze flickered to the woman perched on a vinyl chair. "Don't let her looks deceive you. She might be small, but she packs a mean punch."

Mrs. Langston smiled and lifted her chin. "I'm proud to say after forty-one years of marriage, I'm still going strong."

He turned and gave a nod to his little general. "You mean, *we're* going strong."

"That's right." Her mouth warmed into a grin for her husband. "And so long as you listen to me, we'll keep it that way."

The corners of my mouth lifted. Devotion etched the couple's tone, their gazes loving and supportive, all-knowing yet considerate. I'd seen that kind of connection between my parents, and on some level, had just assumed love would follow that path for me. I hadn't envisioned how gaping potholes and crumbling asphalt would make the road virtually impassable.

"And that's why we're here. Glenn's diabetic, and he has heart issues, too."

Her statement brought my thoughts back to his health. "And how about now, Mr. Langston? Still feeling lightheaded?"

"No."

"Any more shortness of breath?"

"Not since this morning."

His wife waved her index finger. "Show her your heel, Glenn."

"It's nothing. Really."

Mrs. Langston crossed her arms over the purse in her lap. "If nothing is a red, puffy sore that's the size of a silver dollar, then yes, it's *nothing*."

I typed on my computer, adding "possible diabetic ulcer" alongside his vital signs and heart history. When next I looked up, Mrs. Langston had crossed the room to stand beside her husband, hand in his.

I closed my laptop and smiled. "The doctor will be by shortly. In the meantime, may I get you something to drink?"

A few minutes later, after bringing them two bottles of water, I made my way to the nurse's station. I stopped short at the white bakery box on the counter. I peeked inside. *Cinnamon streusel cake.*

I arched an eyebrow at Tiffany. "Don't tell me the new intern's in the doghouse with Naomi again."

"No. It took him long enough, but he finally got with the program."

I leaned a hip on the counter and folded my arms. As happened sometimes with new interns, one would come to the emergency department thinking he—or she—knew best. But that never lasted long with our head nurse. Naomi had been in uniform since before this guy drew his first breath, and she had a knack for taming smug interns.

"Let's just say that now, when Naomi tells him to get over to Trauma Four, he takes off running."

I laughed, glad to hear he was more than a brilliant, curly-haired cricket. "So, who brought the cake?"

"Me, of course."

I turned, sucking in a small breath.

Thorne flashed me his can't-forget-you smile. "I'm not gonna lie. You look a hell of a lot better today than the last time I saw you in this hospital, connected to all those tubes."

As I pulled him into a hug, he held his raincoat aside. I spoke over his ear. "What're you doing here?" I pulled back gently. "Is everything okay…? Jacob?"

"Jacob's fine. Great, actually. I left him with mom, and they're busy in the potting shed. He's probably covered in dirt and—"

"Loving every minute of it, I'll bet," I said, finishing his thought.

He chuckled, then filled me in on the end of his teaching semester and his next historical restoration—an 1850s house in a barrier island town.

"Mom's keeping Jacob for a couple days while I meet with the client."

I smiled. "Which means I'll be staying over with them. I can't wait to see him."

"He'll love that." Thorne pushed his glasses up his nose, glancing at the bustle around the nurse's station. "I know you're busy and all, but could you maybe take a break for a few minutes?"

I knew that tone. I narrowed my gaze, reading the crease in his brow. "Sure, just let me talk to Tiffany, then we can go to the cafeteria."

Minutes later, we were seated in a booth, drinking a couple of diet sodas.

"You're looking better—like you're getting your energy back. Your color."

I tucked a strand of hair behind my ear, content to play along until he was ready to show his cards. "I'm pretty much healed from the accident."

He nodded. "I'm so thankful you were okay. You scared the shit out of me. I don't know what I'd do if something ever happened to you."

My breath hitched, but I managed a quiet, "I'm just glad it's behind me. I'm trying to move on with my life."

"Which is kinda why I'm here."

As silence stretched between us, I heard the sound of his knee bouncing under the table. *I thought you kicked that habit.*

Questions pushed to the front of my mind. Was he worried about me or Jacob? Mom...? Or was it something deeper, like the death of Jacob's mother? Their lost relationship?

I sipped my drink, striving for patience. "Are you trying to make my head hurt?"

"No."

Our gazes met. "You like putting me under a microscope?"

"Of course not."

"That's what this feels like."

"Shit. I'm sorry." He grunted, rubbing the heels of his hands in his eyes before looking at me. "It's just, I don't know. I owe you an apology, Prim. For butting in,

209

for screwing with your life. I hate what I did to you, to Chase. I never should've suggested he be your *somebody*."

I sighed, a little relieved his worry was over something as simple as me. "You were just trying to help. You had no way of knowing I'd had a crush on Chase since I was a kid." I rubbed my hands over my thighs. "Besides, we did this to ourselves. We jumped in too fast. We didn't think things through. I guess we got lost in the feelings and forgot about the facts."

Thorne threaded his fingers together in a fist on the table. "I think Chase is really in love with you."

"I don't want to talk about this."

"But the bigger question in my mind is are you in love with him?"

Inwardly, I flinched. Of course, I loved Chase. I couldn't help it. Beneath the muscle and charm—behind whatever unresolved issues he had with his father and his past—was a kind man with a caring heart…only it was off limits to me.

I wanted to shake my head vigorously in answer to his question, but I could only nod quietly.

"Then you have to give him a chance, Prim. Don't give up. He's dealt with a lot of shit in his life, and he's always used his charm and personality to cover it up."

"Does Chase know you're here?"

"No way."

I leaned back in the booth and stared at the ceiling. "Did he tell you how he came to see me?"

"He did."

"He asked me to marry him." I straightened and caught my brother's gaze. "He actually thought that coming to me with a ring, declaring his love and how he miraculously wants to have a family now, makes everything all right."

"I know him, Prim. He was doing the best he could."

"Well, he came up short. Very short." I sipped my drink, hoping to soothe the desert in my throat. "He doesn't trust me with the truth. And I'm not wasting any more of my time with men who hide behind secrets."

"Did Avery keep secrets from you?"

It was not lost on me that for the first time, my brother didn't refer to him as "Aimless" or "Ass Wipe" or some other derivation.

I nodded, then took a deep breath and folded my arms on the tabletop. "I'm done. Relationships suck. I'm gonna focus on *my* life for a change."

"As you should." He rubbed his fingers over his temple. "But didn't you just admit you love him?"

"Yeah, and I love ice cream, too. But I don't love what it does to my digestive system or my hips."

He nodded, crunching on some ice from his drink.

I tilted my head. "Why does any of this matter to you?"

Moments of heavy silence filled the air before he spoke. "Look, you're my sister. He's my best friend. And when it's clear to me—and to everyone who knows you guys—you're in love with each other, well," he said, glancing at the raindrops tapping on the window, "I just thought you should know he's pretty scared."

"Chase isn't scared." I scoffed. "He just likes having things his way."

He put his hand on my arm. "That's not true. He's scared, Prim. He can't forgive himself."

My gaze narrowed. "What the hell does that even mean?"

Thorne looked past me, the corners of his mouth turned down, as though *he* was the one engaged in the heavyweight bout of the heart. He stretched his neck from side to side and shrugged back his shoulders. "I know I act like an overbearing jackass sometimes, but can you please just trust me on this?"

I blinked, barely breathing, scarcely thinking.

"I know what I'm talking about. Sometimes a person needs to know you forgive him. So he can start to forgive himself."

As I gathered my wits, I questioned—in some tiny measure—whether my brother was talking about Chase or himself.

Chapter Twenty-Two

Tuesday, December 6th 7:30 p.m.
Prim

On the way home from work, I grabbed a carton of praline ice cream from the grocery store, because after my talk with Thorne, I'd tossed everything—including the whole resisting-things-you-love-but-know-are-horrible-for-you philosophy—out the window.

I was tired of always getting tripped up in life.

Tired of always having to be the patient one.

Tired of expectations always dictating my life.

I turned onto my street, humming the chorus of the song I'd sold to Alisha McCall. I wrote "Yesterday Is All I've Got" a few months after Dad died. I was restless with grief, finding avoidance an uncomplicated friend.

While the chorus looped through my head, I parked my car, snatched the grocery sack from the front seat, and walked up my sidewalk. From the corner of my eye, I spotted movement on my front porch, heard footsteps stepping on wood planks. I stopped short. When Chase stepped out of the shadows, I blinked, stunned, but somehow inexplicably relieved.

"How long have you been here?"

"An hour, maybe two. Doesn't matter. There's nothing more important to me than seeing you." Chase shoved his hands in his front pockets. "Did you go for a swim after work?"

I shook my head. "I've been pretty bad about exercising lately."

"Yeah, but with the accident and all—"

"No, it's nothing physical. My doctor says I should go back to life as usual. Trouble is I'm not so sure what that is anymore. I'm still pretty much a mess in here," I said, resting my hand over my heart.

He moved toward me, stopping inches from my toes. "I'm sorry for the pain I've caused you. So damn sorry." His gaze dropped to my mouth and then he blinked away. It took a few seconds before he came back to me. "Look, I know you don't have anything else to say to me. But if you wouldn't mind too much, I have something I need to say to you."

When he raked his hand through his hair, mussing the ends around his collar, I had to make a fist to stop my fingers from tingling.

"When you said I needed to talk to some—"

"Wait. Not out here," I said, pointing to the ice cream carton.

He chuckled under his breath, rubbing his knuckles under his chin. "Yeah, maybe we better go inside."

I slipped out of my coat and shoes, and he followed me to the kitchen, stopping in the doorway and leaning against the frame. I walked to the refrigerator, and after putting the ice cream in the freezer, asked, "Would you like a beer?"

"No thanks. Water's fine." His gaze traveled the room, stopping at the sink. "And how're the pipes doing?"

"Well, I have this great plumber, you see," I said, filling two glasses with ice and water from the tap. "He fixed everything good as new. Maybe you've heard of him…?"

I whipped around, and he gave me a half-baked smile. "Maybe. I'm just glad to hear he took care of you." He cleared his throat then wandered over to the table.

I shook my head at the sight of Chase.

This can't be happening…

This man of cool confidence and easy charisma had just *wandered* across my kitchen like a lost duckling.

"Chase?" His name broke in my throat, a too-tight string snapping on a guitar. I swallowed some water, trying to calm the edge in my voice. "Wanna go in the den?"

"I'll think better in here. Please," he added, gesturing to the chair beside him.

I thudded the glasses on the table, dropped onto the seat, and lifted my gaze. Up close, with my attention solely focused on him, I noticed more changes. His face was thinner, his hair shaggier than usual. Darkness lurked beneath his eyes, the creases around them tentative, needy. I instantly wondered if he could read the same longing in my eyes, too.

Chase held my gaze, skipping the pre-game show. "So. The last time I saw you, you said I needed to talk to someone. You were right, and that's what I did."

I tucked my hair behind my ear. "That's good. *Really* good."

"I talked to Curt. He's been at the center of all my shit for a long time, and I figured it was best to go straight to the source. Talking with anyone else would've been a waste of time."

I blinked, fighting the pulse of emotion flooding my heart. "Wow. Your father?" He nodded. "And how'd it go?"

He chewed on his lower lip for several moments. "You really want to know?"

"Of course."

"Because it's not pretty."

"*Fuck* pretty." I grabbed his arm, giving it a firm squeeze. "A lot's happened between us, but my feelings for you haven't changed—aren't going to change. I just want you to be honest with me."

"Jesus, Prim." He shook his head and groaned. "I don't know…it's ten kinds of fucked up."

"Well, so long as it's not like *twenty* kinds of fucked up, I'm good."

He threw back his head and laughed…really laughed. When his gaze returned to mine, it moved full circle over my forehead, my cheeks, lingering on my mouth.

In that moment, he claimed my heart all over again. I was no longer hurt, in that inward, selfish way. I was…determined. *I'm not letting you go because life just means more when you love.*

"Now. You have something to say to me, and I want to hear it." I laced our fingers together. "Trust me, Chase. Please, just trust me."

He stared me in the eyes and lowered his voice. "Yeah, this is gonna take a while. I think we'd better go in the den."

****

Chase

A knife had been wedged in my gut for most of my life, and somehow—through denial and resiliency—I'd learned to manage it. I skated past relationships, connection, and love by focusing on fly-by-night hookups and my career. Those things made sense to me. I loved women and everything Chase n' Dreams had morphed into over the years. To most, it appeared I navigated life pretty damn well.

It'd taken Prim all of a few months to call bullshit on me.

Just now, as she'd pleaded with me to trust her, the knife twisted deeper in my stomach. Pained, I wanted to retreat, pull her into my arms and kiss her into oblivion. And I could've done it, too. I could tell by the way her lips quivered she wouldn't have stopped me. A lesser man would've done just that.

But I'm not that man anymore.

Sitting on the sofa, I turned my body toward hers, our knees touching. I needed her close, to lean on her while I cracked open the rusty lock on my heart. Prim was a nurturer, a caregiver, and I could sense by the way she watched my face she was calculating how to best support me.

I began with my earliest recollections of Curt, sharing my feelings about abandonment and loneliness, of surviving Mom's death, and nagging feelings of being different from all my friends. I confessed to using women and my nomadic lifestyle to mask my insecurities, how I'd learned early on to use charm to my advantage.

I glanced at the family photo of the Vreeland clan on the coffee table, then looked at Prim. *My Prim.* She was so lovely, so real and natural. *The way morning sunlight kisses a river.* I had to rub my hands on my thighs to keep from touching her, pulling her to me and burying my face in her soft hair.

I took a few deep breaths before bringing up Las

Vegas. This was important, critical to her understanding of who I was before that night, and who I became afterward.

As I began unpacking everything I could remember about Curt, the tattoo, and the vow, I studied her eyes. At times, her blue irises darkened, and at others, they glimmered with wetness. But through it all, her gaze reflected acceptance…and love.

With a pulse of hopefulness, I shifted on the sofa and touched her arm. I explained how I'd gone to see Curt the morning of her accident—gone straight to the source of my disappointment and confusion.

"So, I…" I looked away, unsure about saying this out loud. "Yeah, the thing is…" I rubbed my forehead with my hand before meeting her gaze. "I did it, Prim. I forgave Curt Bova. I fucking forgave him for leaving us, for ignoring me my whole life, for using me as a meal ticket. All of it."

I didn't think it was possible, but with the admission, even more weight slid off my shoulders. I wanted to grab the moment before it grabbed me.

"And I couldn't get home to you fast enough—to tell you I could be the kind of man you wanted and deserved. But then the accident happened—" My voice cracked. "You were hurt and fighting for your life." Before I let myself get lost in the dust of regret, I gave my head a shake. "Look. You didn't want anything to do with me, and I don't blame you."

Silence pulsed around us. I watched a tide of emotions color her face.

"I'm sorry. It hurt too much to see you, and I had to focus on healing."

"You absolutely needed to do that. But I was wrong

to show up at your door with my dog and a ring, expecting you to just take me back. Telling you I'd fixed my problem, solved everything."

Her brow creased. "Is that why you didn't bring Trout with you tonight?"

I nodded. "Explaining all of this was something I needed to do on my own. But honestly, I didn't want to see him get his doggy heart broken again. It took a week for him to get over the last time he saw you. I can't do that to him, you know…if things don't end well for us."

"And how do you feel now?"

"Relieved. Really good, considering I just dumped my ten kinds of fucked up on you."

She leaned her body into the sofa, resting her head on her arm. "You're being too hard on yourself. It wasn't ten…maybe a good six." A smiled teased her mouth, then it softened. "Thank you for trusting me. I wanted to understand what was happening with you—*with us*—but I know it wasn't easy. You hate being vulnerable."

"But I love you."

A smile spread over her lips. "I love you, too."

My chest swelled, and I reached for her hand. "God, I love you so much." I kissed the inside of her wrist, then gazed into her baby blues. "There's not one doubt in my mind you're it for me. I want to spend every day of my life with you and have kids—lots and lots of kids."

Prim blinked, a sheen of tears in her eyes. "I want you—all of you—just as you are."

I tilted her face to mine. "Tell me what else you want."

"I want to go to sleep with you every night and wake up with you spooned around me. I want you to show me the world, Chase. I want to experience people and places and things with you." She paused. "And I want us to build a home and a life together. No matter what comes our way, you're my family. Forever."

"You have me—my whole heart, my soul, everything. I love you now and for the rest of my life. You're all I need."

I spotted the gentle movement of her throat as she swallowed, felt her fingers quivering.

Oh, hell...

"There is one more thing I want." She slid closer, lifting her gaze to mine. "I love you...more now than I ever thought possible. But also, I want to forgive you. I don't really believe there's anything to forgive, but just in case you need it—or want it—you have it." She paused a beat. "I forgive you, Chase."

I lowered my face to her neck and breathed in the scent of her warmth, kindness, and beauty. *Forgiveness.* I had no words to express how complete her gift made me feel. It seemed I'd waited a lifetime for Prim, and I couldn't let another moment pass without her.

I touched my forehead to hers, wrapped my arms around her, and brushed my lips over hers. "Will you marry me, Prim?"

Epilogue

Two Weeks Later
Saturday, Christmas Eve 5:15 p.m.
Prim

My younger brother, Sage, reclined in an upholstered chair across from me, hands folded flat on his chest. Somehow, after all the organized chaos that was my wedding day, we'd found ourselves alone in Mom's bedroom.

Standing in front of the full length mirror, I gazed at my reflection. The white crepe A-line dress had a classic boat neckline and long sleeves with a fitted silhouette. My sister, Billie, had styled my hair into a chignon with two simple pearl combs.

"You look gorgeous." Sage waggled his eyebrows at me in the mirror and added, "But then you'd look beautiful in a flour sack, so what do I know?"

I gave him a slow smile. "You really have a way with words."

"Yeah, well it's a good thing since I write TV scripts for a living." He stretched out his legs, crossing his feet at the ankles. "Which makes me think I really should've gone hunting for plotlines in my family's love lives years ago."

I glared at him through the mirror.

"What…?" he asked, as innocently as when he was

four and demanded to know why he couldn't have a third piece of Christmas fudge before bedtime. "I'm just saying, I couldn't have written a better story if I tried. You, Chase, a secret crush. Really good stuff." He steepled his hands under his chin. "Fast forward to a whirlwind romance, intense breakup. Then finally the couple reunites, the bride pulling together a wedding in just two weeks." He wagged his finger at me. "Now that's award-winning stuff right there."

"Ha. Ha." I turned around, placing my hand gently but firmly on my waist. "Don't you have somewhere else to be?"

He wrinkled his brow. "Nope. You gave me the best job of all, remember? Mom's easy."

Hm, you're right about that. As I watched a grin stretch across his mouth, I ticked through the wedding party one last time.

As had been the tradition with both my sisters' weddings, Ace was giving me away.

Thorne, best man.

Goldie, matron of honor. *Check, check, check.*

Billie and Carrie, bridesmaids.

Chloe and Charlotte, flower girls. Jacob, ring bearer. *Check, check, and more checks.*

And last, but never least, Sage.

My brother's job was walking Mom down the aisle, sitting by her side—in short, being her anchor. *But Sage is right.* Mom was easy, calm and steady, thrilled about the marriage and not the slightest bit nervous.

Sage rose from his chair and walked to the window, staring out. I joined him, and he took my hand, and we gazed at family and friends gathering for the ceremony. I spotted Tiffany and Brent…and the Chase n' Dreams crew, too. I smiled when I glimpsed Grandma Vreeland wearing a simple balsam green dress and sitting on the front row. Then, my mouth twitched when I saw Ace's often absent girlfriend take a seat alongside her.

Megan was a magazine journalist who spent weeks at a time on the road for her job. I figured Christmas Eve was most likely the only reason she was here at all. That, and well, hopefully, to be with my brother for the holiday.

As she tossed her hair behind her back and checked her watch, my pulse spiked. "I honestly don't know what Ace sees in her."

Sage chuckled, turning his gaze in my direction. "I know, right? Sure, she's pretty and smart, but she also—"

"—Looks so *preoccupied* all the time. Like there's something else she'd rather be doing. Like cleaning her refrigerator."

"Or getting her roots dyed."

I laughed, his remark reminding me why he was so good at his work. His imagination was endless. He was such a great observer of people, pinpoint accurate when it came to peeling back the layers of a person's character.

I looked at my brother and grinned. "Thank you for always making me laugh." I thought it over more. "And thank you, Sage, for making my wedding day so beautiful."

He squeezed my hand. "You're welcome. I just took your vision and brought it to life. We do it all the time with the sets on the show." He tipped his head to heaven. "But honestly, we have to thank God for the beautiful day."

Sage was right. Winter days like this one were a gift

from Him.

My gaze followed the crimson beams from the setting sun as they spilled over rows of white folding chairs in our back yard. Lush red poinsettias lined the aisle, and candles and luminarias flickered a soft glow. And beneath the tree that was once home to The Hideout, stood a white trellis draped with greenery and red berries.

I wiggled my toes inside my pearl buckle flats, memories of those slick-bottomed sneakers never too far away. "You don't think it's silly, do you? Getting married outdoors on Christmas Eve, underneath our tree?"

"Hell, no. I love it. Like I said, it doesn't get much better than this." My brother turned to me, taking a gentler tone. "Hey. All kidding aside, I'm so happy for you, Prim. You've always been there for me—for all of us. It's time for us to be here for you." He took a deep breath. "You and Chase have been through a lot. True. But you came out together, as one, on top. We should all be so lucky to get that kind of happy ending."

"Wow…that was really beautiful. Thanks, Sage. I love you."

My brother leaned down and pressed a kiss to my head.

"Knock, knock," Goldie said, grinning as she entered the bedroom.

Sage and I shared a knowing smile, then greeted our sister.

Goldie rubbed her hands over my sleeves. "Are you about ready? There happens to be a *highly* motivated groom downstairs just waiting to make you his bride."

Ace stepped in beside Goldie, tugging gently at the tie around his neck. "More like chomping at the bit.

Never seen a guy quite so happy on his wedding day."

My skin hummed and my pulse quickened at the thought of becoming Chase's wife. *Flip a holy pancake.* I'll have him, and he'll have me, for the rest of our lives. Forever...

Ace hooked his arm playfully around Sage's neck. "Hey, it's show time, little brother. Mom's waiting for you downstairs."

Sage gave me a wink, kissed my hand, then followed Goldie out the door.

Ace turned to me, drawing in a breath. "You're so beautiful, Prim. Absolutely perfect. You know there's no way I will ever believe any man is good enough for you, right?" I nodded. "Now, I'm going to ask you the same question I asked Billie and Goldie on their wedding days."

I held my breath.

"Do you love Chase? Are you ready to marry him, commit to him for the rest of your life?"

I answered without hesitation. "Yes, and yes."

"I like it. Short and sweet. Just like this wedding." Smiling, he gave me the crook of his arm. "Now, what do you say we get you married?"

We took a few steps, then I stopped. "Wait. How did Billie answer?"

His brow creased. "She said, 'Of course. I'm young, Ace. Not stupid.'"

I laughed, and before I could ask, he added, "And Goldie. She gave me a high five and said, 'Hell, yeah.'"

Yep. Sounds like my sisters.

A few minutes later, Ace and I were waiting, watching the others in the wedding party make their way down the aisle. Violin music filled the air, but everything faded away when we stepped outside, and my gaze locked on Chase. He wore a black tuxedo with a white rose in his lapel. He looked so stunning my breath got all tangled up in my chest.

I trusted Ace to get me to the trellis, and moments later, I felt him kiss my cheek and place my hand in Chase's larger one.

Then, the reverend began to speak.

And after that, Chase.

"I never loved anyone until you," he began. "I didn't think I was worthy of love, but you, you changed all of that. You took the darkness out of my life and filled it with light. You're my home, and I thank God every day for bringing you to me. You have me, Prim. I love you today. I love you between today and someday. I'll love you forever."

I tilted my head to the branches above us. "I was eight years old when you saved me from falling out of this tree, and even then I knew you were special." As I lowered my gaze to him, a tear slipped past my lashes. "You were gentle and kind. And now, you're all those things and more. Your love supports me and encourages me…challenges me. I have faith in us, and I know whenever we take a leap in life, we'll do it together, holding each other's hand. You have me, Chase. I love you today. I love you between today and someday. I'll love you forever."

Chase bent his head, and I closed my eyes. Then the reverend lightly cleared his throat. "Sorry, Chase. It's not time for *that* yet."

As my soon-to-be husband gazed into my eyes, I thought about life. *Choices.* About how you made a good one, then a bad one. How you'd make a questionable one, then another bad one. But none of them mattered because in the end, living a life with love meant rolling up your sleeves, regrouping, and having a go at it again.

"With all due respect, Reverend, I was hoping you could just catch up with me." A smile reached Chase's whiskey brown eyes. " 'Cause I'm already there."

With that, pure joy spread through my heart. I knew today—and every day from here on—would be our *someday*.

A word about the author...

Ann enjoys spending time with family, trying out new recipes, and relaxing on her back porch to read and write. She's a member of Heart of Carolina Romance Writers. She loves watching television dramas and always has a great romance book in her hand. For all the latest, connect with Ann and join her reader group at https://annmtrader.com/newsletter/